Blood
Upon The
Snow

By
Bryndon Wenger

Dedicated to my beloved wife, Emily.

Contents

Prologue

Under pregnant skies and a moonless night, the earth shook to the pounding of rainfall and rolling thunder. The sound of running hooves became dormant to the howling screams of ghosts in the fog. My heart raced to the beat of hooves upon the leaves below. My breath quivered against the rumble of shattering winds pressed against my chest.

I could feel my heart pounding in my ears. My skin felt cold in the chill of the night. A piercing pain shot down my neck and into my chest.

"Live!" I said to myself.

"Just a little further," I told myself as my stallion raced to carry me back to my castle.

The silhouette of my acropolis rose against the sky like the outstretched pillars of Erechtheion. As I passed through the gate, everything turned black. No more pain. No more fear. Just peace and calm.

Then I woke up. I found myself in my room in my bed. I could hear the distant call of my name.

"Nathelia," called out a disembodied voice.

The voice sounded familiar, but I didn't know where it came from. As I climbed from bed, I began to feel a pull against me as if my feet were not my own. I could feel myself being carried out of my room and into the main hall. Looking at my feet, I started seeing pools of crimson that dabbled the floor under a sea of corpses. Looking toward the end of the hall stood a familiar silhouette of a woman whom I hadn't seen in several ages.

"Mom?" I called, but my voice did not emanate from my own lips. It sounded distant and hollow, an echo.

The familiar figure passed into an adjacent room. She seemed to almost float, her dress billowing around her in the wind. Even as I tried to run away, I could once again feel a pull carrying me towards her. My foot placed itself before the other, making its way toward her. As I entered the Grand Hall, I could clearly see, as she stood in front of a window and was showered by the rays of moonlight, that it was, in fact, my mother. How could this be? I had lost her to consumption nearly 12 summers before.

"H-how...I saw you-" I exclaimed.

"Die?" she asked. Her voice was one I remembered, but it sounded as if it encapsulated me. Her voice came not just from her, it came from the walls, the arches, the doorways.

"Yes...I-how?" I proclaimed.

"Correct, my dearest Nathelia," she answered. "My death was only the beginning of a life so extravagant that bibles and holy men couldn't possibly fathom its splendor."

"But if you died, then how are you here?" I asked while choking back tears.

"Before I died, I was approached by a man who offered me a second chance at life, but there was a catch," my mother said.

"A catch? A man? A second chance?" I cried out in confusion.

"Yes, the man was a traveler by the name Corvainius. And the catch was that I had to leave behind the life I once knew for the safety of all I had loved," she explained.

"But how could you just move on without telling anyone? Without telling me?" I cried aloud.

"I knew your father couldn't simply stay away," she said.

"But my father, your husband, died in a hunting accident-," I replied.

"No, dear, I was there when he died," she answered, so calm and poised.

"Wha-," I stammered.

"Like I said, your father couldn't stay away," she declared.

"WHAT HAPPENED TO HIM? WHAT HAPPENED TO MY FATHER," I screamed. "TELL ME."

"After I was given a second chance, I knew what I had to do, but it was so difficult to stay away, and once your father saw me in a crowd, I had to make a choice," she explained.

"What were your choices?" My voice shook now, reverberating through my entire body.

"Either kill him or make him like me," she answered.

I felt a choking sensation as I fought back tears and rage. A rising sickness formed in my stomach.

"WHAT DID YOU DO? WHY DID YOU KILL HIM?" I screamed.

"She didn't kill me," said another familiar voice from behind me.

I spun around to see a man I once knew before, a man who became lost to me.

"Hello, Nathelia," he said with a calming smile.

All I wanted to do was to collapse into his arms and weep like an infant, but I couldn't find the strength to move. His arms coiled around me in a tight embrace.

"What kind of dream is this? I need to wake up," I began demanding aloud.

"This isn't a dream, my dear," said both of my parents in unison.

"If you couldn't be here then, how are you here now?" I asked.

"You're becoming like us," my mother stated.

"What is this? Some kind of sick dream?" I demanded.

They looked at each other and then into my eyes. In unison, they said, "No, dear. You're dying."

Chapter 1:
Greeting Summers Embrace

It was 646 in the year of our lord. Summer was the time of my birth. The sun beat down on the backs of farmers and maidens in the fields. The air outside carried the smells of fresh-cut hay and manure. Atop a precipice stood a castle of such magnificence that even Olympus paled in comparison. A throng of doves encircled the summit.

Inside the castle, a grand celebration was afoot. From every banister hung majestic tapestries. Each carried the castle's coat of arms. The sound of parade trumpets carried echoes of joy throughout the halls. In a corner, towards the edge of the castle, tucked away, was a mother getting ready to bring a child into the world.

For hours, midwives paced up and down the halls carrying basins of water and fresh linen. My mother was a beautiful, dark-haired woman with piercing hazel eyes that could weaken the souls of most men with a single glance. Even as a woman of smaller stature, my mother still carried herself with a grace that commanded respect and honor. The name my mother carried was Queen Jezebel. She was with child shortly before being betrothed to my father, King Marcus.

They seemed to be the most notorious couple the world had yet to know. In the eyes of the world, there were no two beings that could have possibly loved each other the way my parents did. I was a secret that was meant to be taken to the grave. Since my parents were not yet married, I was a child out of wedlock.

Rumors never became closed-door whispers because everyone admired the love that my parents displayed for each other. I can't recall a time when my father did not worship the ground upon which my mother walked. They were thought of as having an envied love that was only described in fables and children's tales. Their love was the love of dreams, which brought joy and hope to all of the lands.

Before becoming a queen, my mother was merely a fair maiden of a small town outside the limits of the castle's reach called Glovendall. It wasn't a town of splendor like others. Glovendall was a town of silk weavers and fabric makers. At the young age of eighteen, my father found himself wandering the streets of Glovendall looking for anyone who could design and produce a banner that would bring hope to his parents' kingdom after both of them were sent off for war, leaving my father, Marcus, behind to tend to the affairs of the kingdom in their absence.

Joy was beginning to fade, and hope was all but lost, and something needed to be done. Upon his inquisition to find what he had sought, Marcus had caught a glimpse of an auburn-haired beauty- divinity's creature. The beat of his heart began to thunder loudly like a raging storm. The sheer magnificence of this maiden could shatter the ice off even the most frozen of hearts.

She was sitting at a loom in a white dress, weaving fibers of silk into fabric. Marcus found himself in admiration. Her hands looked as smooth as porcelain. As her fingers danced along the fibers with grace and rhythm, Marcus could do nothing more than stare, seemingly held in place by her powerful pull. He watched as her hands caressed the fibers and teased them into a weave. As Marcus watched, fascinated by this woman's elegance, he found it hard to breathe, and his palms began to sweat. If he had never known love before, this was it.

"Can I help you with something?" the maiden asked through a hint of laughter.

"I'm sorry. I don't mean to stare, but-" replied Marcus.

"I'm guessing you have never seen a fabric being woven," she inquired.

"No…I mean, yes, but-" he stammered.

"Then what is it that makes you so rude?" she fired back.

"It's just that I have never seen someone with such beauty and grace weave such majestic fabrics," replied Marcus.

"You mean to tell me you don't have a weaver in your castle?" she asked arrogantly.

"Wait, how did you know-" Marcus began to reply.

"I could smell the royalty on you from miles away," she stated, cutting off Marcus.

"So you know I'm a…" Marcus started.

"A spoiled rich kid?" the maiden snapped back.

"For your information, I happen to be the prince," he demanded.

"For your information-" mocked the maiden, moving her head from side to side and pointing a needle at Marcus.

"Here in Glovendall, you are nothing more than a rude, pompous ass with a complex," she continued with a smile.

Marcus puffed out his chest and stood a bit straighter. "My name is Marcus. The prince of Glaradon," he stated.

"And my name is Jezebel. State your business here quickly, for I have found myself quite busy without a reserve of time for the likes of royalty," she said with a hint of defiance.

No matter the aggression towards Marcus, he couldn't shake his lustful desire for her. Never in Marcus' young life had he dreamt of a feeling such as this. For the common folk to have spoken to Marcus in this manner would have been a death sentence. But not for Jezebel. She was different. Her sassiness and reserve only further illuminated a spark hidden deep within Marcus.

"I am here to ask you to accompany me back to the castle and weave a banner that can bring hope to the people of my kingdom," Marcus stated.

"Since Glovendall is not part of your kingdom, what if I refuse?" she asked.

"I have the authority of my father, the king, to take you by force," Marcus declared.

"Your authority only pertains to your kingdom, and you have no power here," Jezebel stated matter-of-factly.

She was not wrong. Marcus felt his shoulders slumping. He looked to the side and thought for a minute before saying, "Please, I beg of you."

Jezebel stood from her loom, and Marcus's breath was taken away once more. The way the fabric of her dress fell against her caused Marcus' heart to beat to the sound of a thousand thundering horses. In the sunlight, Jezebel's dress seemed almost translucent as it hung tightly to her hips and the firm curvature of her taunt bosom. Marcus couldn't even dream of encountering such majestic beauty. His mind began to swim through a raging sea of emotions and lust, causing his knees to become weak.

"What's in it for me?" Jezebel asked.

"You will weave me a banner, and both you and your family will be cared for by the kingdom and its subjects," Marcus answered.

"Okay," said Jezebel, and began to skip with childish glee.

Marcus found himself dumbfounded and confused. He opened and closed his mouth in dubiety, unsure what he could say. Jezebel ran inside her cottage and bid farewell to her parents with a hug and a kiss. Jezebel's house was merely a small stone cottage with a thatched roof. Flowers hung in a wooden box under each window. Large flat stones paved the walkway to the entrance.

A few moments later, Jezebel began skipping towards the carriage with a girlish gait. Marcus watched as she came toward him. He had been admiring the braids in one of his horses; now the horse itself seemed to stiffen upon noticing the beautiful girl approaching. Her simple innocence and potential for brash conflict only forged Marcus' feelings for her even stronger.

Marcus went into the carriage, standing at the door and putting a hand out for her to take. She did, and he felt the softness of her skin. She smiled as he climbed into the carriage and kept pointing outside the window as they rode.

Jezebel had never ventured outside the confines of Glovendall. As she began to travel with Marcus and his soldiers, the world became a fantastic wonder.

She gazed from inside the carriage in complete bewilderment. As the landscape passed by her window, colorful birds danced overhead high above the treetops. She gazed upon lush green fields being teased in the wind by a flock of butterflies. The air was saturated with the smells of sweet grass and wildflowers.

As night fell, Marcus ordered a halt to their travels and began setting up camp. The carriage had stopped on a forest trail that was carpeted by soft grass and spongy moss. Upon exiting the carriage, Jezebel was engulfed by the sounds of nature. The sound of birds singing was accented by the buzzing of insects and the orchestrated crescendo of wind in the rustling trees. The sound of a brook could be heard in the distance.

"I'm going to the brook to bathe," Jezebel said.

"You must stay with us-" said a soldier, drawing a sword from his scabbard.

Marcus gestured for the soldiers to stand down and told her to go ahead.

"My apologies, your royal highness," pleaded the soldier, sheathing his sword and standing at ease.

After a short time, Marcus began to walk toward the brook, leaving the soldiers behind to continue setting up camp. After a brief trek, Marcus found himself at the brook and hid behind a tree, out of sight of the bathing Jezebel. He watched in lustful bewilderment as she stood in the shallow brook. Her hair lay thickly over her shoulders, exposing her back and firm, apple-shaped buttocks. As the water fell from her body, it looked like diamonds falling from flawless porcelain.

Jezebel turned herself toward the bank, exposing her perky breast with firm pink nipples. Her stomach was toned and smooth, untouched from being with a child. A small tuft of pubic hair lay against her like spring moss upon a snowy stone. As Marcus gazed upon her and the exquisite beauty she beheld, his trousers began to grow tight from his engorgement.

As if captured by a spell, his hand began to caress his shame. As much as he thought he was hidden from sight, Jezebel spotted him.

"You know I can see you," said Jezebel. Marcus became frozen in fear and embarrassment. His heart raced with lustful anxiety.

"Step out here and face me," demanded Jezebel. Marcus stepped from behind the tree with his hands covering his engorgement.

"Remove your hands and accept your shame like the fearless prince that you are!" Jezebel declared. As Marcus moved his hands aside, Jezebel stepped from the water and onto the bank, and glistening droplets fell at her feet. As she stepped towards him, she stopped within inches of him. Marcus's hands began to tremble, and his body quivered in anxiousness, which brought a smile to Jezebel's face. "What is it that you wish for me?" asked Jezebel softly.

"I wish to have you as my own," Marcus murmured.

"Then take me, your royal highness," declared Jezebel. With quivering hands, Marcus gently placed one hand on the back of her neck and the other on her waist. Pulling her close, with her arm stretched behind his neck, he pressed his lips to hers, and his heart began to pound loudly against her chest. His hands began to trace the curvature of her back.

Jezebel began to viscously tear away Marcus's clothing. Through a strong embrace, Marcus gently lowered Jezebel upon a bed of moss along the bank. He gazed into her eyes as they twinkled like a rare gem, dancing in the reflection of the water. Jezebel's hair smelled of lavender and spring breeze.

Marcus began to kiss her neck, causing Jezebel to release a subtle moan from deep within her chest. His lips traced along her breasts, and his tongue began to circle around the jaunty flesh of her nipples. Jezebel's leg began to caress Marcus's waist. As he began to drag his lips towards her hips, Jezebel's body began to quiver with excitement. Marcus inhaled deeply the erotic scents of her body. His tongue teased the taunt flesh between her legs, causing Jezebel to release a lascivious gasp of pleasure. She buried her hands into his hair, pressing him against her hips. Marcus sat up and leaned forward, inserting himself into her, causing both of them to gasp in ecstasy.

With every thrust of his hips, he could feel Jezebel's nails digging deeper into his back. They both gazed into each other's eyes while in erotic bliss. Jezebel threw her head back and released what seemed to be an involuntary scream. While digging deeply into Marcus's flesh, Jezebel rolled Marcus onto his back, raising and lowering her body against his. Jezebel dragged her nails along Marcus's chest, causing him to groan a lustful moan. Jezebel threw her body erect, clutching her breasts, and screamed.

The echoes of their lustful pleasure carried against the rocks of the brook and drifted into the vast expanse of forest surrounding them. After both of them reached the climax, Jezebel collapsed onto Marcus's chest. Breathing heavily, both Marcus and Jezebel lay along the bank, embracing one another.

"I love you," whispered Marcus with labored breath.

"You hardly know me," replied Jezebel.

"Yet I feel as though I have known you all of my life because it has been entwined with yours," Marcus said.

"I felt a pull to you when I first laid eyes on you," stated Jezebel.

"I do not believe encountering one another was a mere coincidence. I believe fate has had a hand at play," Marcus replied.

"If this is fate indeed, then may destiny continue to bless us forever more," proclaimed Jezebel.

Whether or not fate brought Marcus and Jezebel together, one thing was for certain: their hearts had become bonded through the forges of passion. The dawning of their love was the covet of Himeros.

"I wish to have you by my side until the end of time," said Marcus.

"As you wish," replied Jezebel.

Both Marcus and Jezebel lay on the mossy floor, embracing each other as they listened to the sounds of nature, which enveloped them for what seemed like an eternity.

"Your mesmerizing beauty captivates me," Marcus spoke softly, not to disturb the chorus of nature around them.

"I am captivated by the security of your arms. If this is to be my future, then may I be carried on the wings of destiny. But if this is merely a fleeting moment, I pray that the sun never sets," whispered Jezebel.

After a period of time, both Jezebel and Marcus redressed and began heading back to camp.

"Is everything alright, your highness?" asked a soldier.

"Everything is exactly as it should be," replied Marcus as both Marcus and Jezebel looked at each other and smiled. As the sun began to fade behind the horizon, Marcus ordered the soldier to make a fire for them. The sounds of the night came alive around them as the men worked merrily humming a tune. But Jezebel's eyes were wide, focused upon a figure in the trees.

A bloodcurdling scream from Jezebel shattered the tranquility of the night. The soldiers jumped to their feet with swords drawn and ready.

"What is it? What's wrong?" stammered Marcus.

"I saw a man standing over there in the trees," screamed Jezebel.

With a single motion from Marcus, the soldiers spread out to search the area. After a short time, all but one of the soldiers returned. Upon the discovery of a soldier missing, tension grew in the air, and a stillness flooded the forest. Everyone waited at the campsite for the missing soldier to return. The only sound that could be heard was the rhythmic breathing of soldiers.

"Shall we go after him, your highness?" asked one of the soldiers.

"No, stay here and keep watch," ordered Marcus, who had a sense of uneasiness in his voice.

Jezebel and Marcus retired for the night, but little did Jezebel know the horrors of the night had just begun. While she slept, a terrifying nightmare began to emerge. Jezebel began to dream of the forest, dark and cold, full of fog. In her dream, she could feel the chill of the air that sent shivers down her spine.

The fire had become embers, and the night was still. Standing in the distance was the tall figure of a man. The same figure she had witnessed earlier. Jezebel could feel her hair begin to stand on end. Her heart began to pound fast and heavy in her chest. A distant voice came from the figure.

"*Come to me,*" whispered the figure.

"Who are you?" Jezebel called out.

"*Come to me,*" the figure whispered again.

"Did you hear me? I asked who you were," Jezebel demanded.

With an unseen force, Jezebel began to levitate off the forest floor and was being carried towards the mysterious figure. As Jezebel approached closer, it became clear that the figure was indeed a man. His hair was long and black. He was wearing aged clothing that was dirty with dark-colored stains. His trousers stopped at his knees with white stockings and leather boots.

His skin was pale, and his eyelids were dark around the edges. His lips looked cold and blue in the moonlight. Dark veins stretched along his cheeks like the web of a spider. His eyes had a piercing, inhuman glow. His hands were dirty, and his fingernails were overgrown. He wore an onyx-studded ring on his left hand. In his hand, he carried a black cane that held a ruby on top. He wore a burgundy velvet tunic and a deeply stained ruffle. For clothing so dingy, his style suggested he was of elegance and nobility.

A dark substance stained the corners of his lips. His clothes smelled of wet earth and decay. The spinal shivers that Jezebel had felt grew into tremors. Jezebel felt paralyzed by fear and helplessness.

The man who stood before her smiled, revealing razor-sharp fangs at each corner of his mouth.

"Who-who are you, and what do you want with me?" stuttered Jezebel.

"My name is Corvainius, and you will be mine," answered the man.

And with a glass-shattering scream, Jezebel woke. Sitting up abruptly and drenched in sweat, Jezebel's body began to quake uncontrollably. Her skin was cold and clammy, and her hair clung to her saturated clothing.

Marcus started awake and sprang to his feet in terror.

"W-what's wrong?" stammered Marcus. He shook her shoulders, trying to get her out of her daze. "My dear, are you alright?"

"I-I saw him," Jezebel stammered in fear.

"Who?" Marcus asked.

"Corvainius. He said his name was Corvainius," exclaimed Jezebel.

Jezebel stared off into the forest as her entire body continued to tremble. Marcus could see the droplets of sweat beginning to pool around her clavicle, glide down her neck, and disappear between her breasts. It reminded Marcus of how it looked like diamonds and how radiant Jezebel was. Even though Jezebel was disheveled, Marcus could not help but stare as her beauty took his breath away. Marcus embraced her and guided her into lying down again. And with a gentle kiss on her forehead and devoted reassurance, Jezebel closed her eyes and fell back asleep.

Marcus lay awake beside Jezebel and held her as he listened to the sounds of her breathing beginning to soften. Her shaking began to reduce as she slipped into a slumber with faint shivers of residual terror. Hours had passed, and the sun began to rise.

Marcus watched as Jezebel opened her eyes and smiled at him.

"Didn't you go back to sleep?" she asked.

"No, I couldn't bear the thought of closing my eyes and not seeing you there," answered Marcus.

Jezebel's eyes shone in the morning light like a frozen lake of gold. As she smiled, her teeth glistened like fresh snow. As Marcus looked upon her, he became entranced by the glowing halo of sunlight around her hair. A small portion of her hair had fallen over her right eye, and Marcus used his hand to brush it over her ear gently. Marcus leaned in for a kiss but was interrupted by a soldier frantically entering the tent.

Startled by the intrusion, Jezebel quickly covered herself with a blanket made from fur.

"My apologies, your highness," said the soldier.

"What is it?" asked Marcus.

"You see… Well, that soldier, last night, he's back!" the soldier exclaimed.

"But he's uh…Well," stammered the soldier.

"Well…Where is he? Move aside, I will see for myself," commanded Marcus.

The soldier stepped aside to make room for Marcus to throw back the entrance cover to the tent and step out into the forest. Marcus saw the soldiers gathered around a tree. As Marcus pushed his way to the middle of the crowd of soldiers, he saw the one missing soldier lying on the ground, struggling to speak and spitting blood with every word. The soldier was a young man with brown hair and blue eyes. These weren't the eyes of a dangerous man. Instead, they were the eyes of a boy who had a loving mother back home.

His eyes were accented by a gentle field of freckles that traced the contour of his nose. His face carried the faint stubble of a man. His skin was pale gray, and his lips were light blue and smeared with blood. His face was drenched in sweat, and a violent heat radiated from his body. A large, tearing wound was salient on the side of his neck. Marcus knelt down and clutched the soldier's hand tightly, knowing the end was near.

"Who did this to you?" Marcus petitioned.

"B-b-b-beast," said the soldier as his voice gurgled.

Between each labored breath, the soldier coughed garnet drops of blood. It seemed like a ruby stream that trickled from the corners of his lips.

"What is your name?" asked Marcus.

"Izak…your(cough)…royal-" the soldier tried to answer.

"Shhh-" whispered Marcus.

"I…don't…want…to die… without honor," Izak chokingly pleaded.

With every cough of blood, Izak gripped tighter to Marcus's hand.

"You carry more honor than most men," replied Marcus.

Marcus laid his own sword upon Izak's chest. Marcus's father had taken the sword off the body of King Toren in the battle of the crowns. The sword was unique in itself. The handle was a silver neck and head of a dragon studded in diamonds and a single ruby laced in each eye. The hilt held the shape of the wings. The blade of the sword formed the winding tail of the dragon. Izak gripped the sword tightly and held it close to his chest.

"Thank you, your hi…highne- said Izak as he took his final breath. Marcus placed his hands over Izak's eyes to close them and bowed his head to pray. Behind Marcus stood Jezebel in complete shock, with tears flowing down her cheeks. Marcus stood and embraced her, holding her tightly. Marcus could feel her tears absorbing into his tunic. As Jezebel sobbed upon his chest, Marcus did his best to soothe her afflictions.

"IT WAS HIM! IT WAS HIM!" cried Jezebel as her voice was stifled in Marcus's chest.

"My dear, I promise you that I will catch the being responsible for this," Marcus reassured.

The soldiers wrapped Izak's body in linen and carried him down by the brook. His body was placed atop a large pyre to be burned. After the pyre was ignited, raging flames crept towards the heavens. Izak's body disappeared in the bulk of flames and smoke. Marcus looked at Jezebel and watched the reflection of the flames shine in her eyes.

Tears flowed down her cheeks as she looked on in silence. After the flames died down to embers, Marcus ordered the soldiers to dismantle the camp and prepare to carry on with their journey back to the castle. For the duration of the journey, Jezebel sat quietly gazing out the window of the carriage.

"What is it, my dear?" inquired Marcus.

"I can't shake the thought of that man from my mind," she stated.

"It was merely a dream," Marcus responded.

"It was much more than a dream; it feels more like a premonition," Jezebel pleaded.

"There, there, my dear, you have nothing to fear. Look, we have reached the castle," reassured Marcus.

Chapter 2:
A Crown of Rust

Marcus was born into the splendor of royalty, the son of the revered King and Queen of Glaradon. But his father's path to the throne was paved with blood. The crown had once belonged to Marcus's uncle who had been a valiant ruler. He met his end in the brutal and historic Battle of the Crowns. Slain by the ruthless King Toren, his death ignited a fire of vengeance in Marcus's father, who reclaimed both the throne and his brother's honor—using the very sword that had taken his life.

Princehood was, at first, not what Marcus wanted. He longed for the carefree joys of childhood, but his noble birthright meant that he always had to act as a future king would. He was not allowed outside the wall of the castle for the first decade of his life. So, he found moments of escape within the castle walls, laughing and clashing wooden swords with the other children.

Marcus's mother would become disgruntled when seeing Marcus galavanting with children from outside the castle.

"We do not settle ourselves amongst the commoners of the kingdom," Marcus's mother viciously declared.

"If we are not to settle amongst them, then how are they to be loyal to the crown?" pleaded Marcus.

"You will learn the purpose of your title in due time," snapped the Queen.

"I want to have friends and go on adventures like you and Father," cried Marcus.

"It is not your place to make such decisions," said the Queen.

"Then what is my place, mother?" Marcus snapped back.

"Your place is to do what you're told and follow the order of the kingdom," replied the Queen indignantly.

"One of these days, I will rule this kingdom as I see fit," declared Marcus.

With a swift backhand and a cracking clap against Marcus's cheek, the conversation was over.

"Now go get changed. Your father is expecting you at court," the Queen said.

"Yes, Mother, of course," replied Marcus, caressing the pain on his cheek.

"Uh-um," said the Queen, clearing her throat.

"Yes, your Majesty," Marcus corrected.

"Now that's better. Give your mother a kiss and run along," stated the Queen.

With a fleeting kiss on his mother's cheek, Marcus ran inside to change clothes. Marcus was a boy of average build and blonde hair. Marcus's eyes were a frosty blue. His skin was smooth and fair. At the age of ten, Marcus towered over most children his age. Upon his tenth birthday, his parents assigned him to the care of a knight named Aedon to teach him how to wield a sword. Aedon seemed terrifying for a knight. He towered over most men and carried a large broadsword that was littered with chips from countless fearless battles.

His armor was as black as a midnight sky. It blended with his long black hair that was always unkempt but rested upon his shoulders. A scar lay across his left eye, leaving it cloudy and white. His right eye was a dark brown but looked nearly black in color. This was the eye that seemed to bear into his soul every time Marcus practiced with a sword. A battle scar stretched from the bottom of

Aedon's lip to his chin. Across Aedon's jaw lay unshaven stubble. Marcus thought to himself that each fiber of stubble symbolized each child Aedon had devoured.

"How much do you know about a sword boy?" asked Aedon with a voice so cold it could freeze hell.

"Enough to defend myself from the likes of-" stated Marcus arrogantly.

"Prepare yourself," declared Aedon, throwing a wooden sword to Marcus.

Marcus caught the sword, holding it up before him.

"Ready," Aedon said. Marcus had barely got through his nod when blackness came bearing down on him.

With the speed of lightning and one quick move, Marcus found himself disarmed and on his back, gasping for air.

"You know nothing of a sword," Aedon stated.

"Y-Yes, I do," said Marcus as he stood, trying to regain his breath.

"Then show me," Aedon demanded.

Marcus raised the wooden sword high, and in the blink of an eye, he once again found himself on the ground, gasping for air.

"Again," said Aedon.

"My mother is -" wheezed Marcus while attempting to regain his footing.

Without warning, Marcus felt a blow to his stomach that sent him reeling in mid-air, and a flash of white filled his vision. Marcus lay on the ground, unwilling to move as his body was flooded with pain.

"When you are ready, the real training will begin," Aedon stated.

Marcus fought back tears from the pain that covered his body. He sat upright and exhaled deeply, using the wooden sword to bring himself to his feet.

"I am ready to learn," groaned Marcus through labored breathing.

"Well then, first, we have to correct your stance," said Aedon.

Aedon used his boot to part and set Marcus for a proper stance.

"Keep your leg back," ordered Aedon while pushing on Marcus's chest.

"This way, you will not fall back so easily," Aedon continued. Marcus winced in pain as he listened to the instructions.

"Now, hold your sword in front of you to guard your chest," said Aedon.

Marcus extended his arms out, holding the sword forward.

Aedon placed one finger under the sword and raised the tip of Marcus's sword to display proper posture.

"A sword is both a shield and a weapon," Aedon informed as he circled Marcus, monitoring his posture. "It can either save your life or end others."

With a firm horizontal swing, Aedon struck Marcus's sword, once again disarming him, though this time, Marcus did not fall.

"The result that you should desire is to disarm your enemy," informed Aedon as he put his sword in its sheath. "When you have done that, you will have gained the upper hand."

The young boy looked at Aedon with fierce determination in his eyes. "Again," he said, scurrying over to pick up his lost weapon.

Aedon let out a deep breath, a smile playing on the corners of his lips.

As the days grew, Marcus found himself determined to disarm Aedon and continued to practice for hours a day. Days turned into weeks, and weeks grew into months, and months turned into years. Marcus continued training tirelessly for hours until, one day, he knew he had what it took. He was determined to show Aedon the same.

It was a warm summer's afternoon. The two were sparring in the courtyard. Marcus held his own against Aedon, dodging his attacks, getting in quick blows before darting away and never once being hit himself.

The larger man was sweating; his movements had become sluggish since they had been sparring for a while now. Still, he gave it his all, sending heavy blows toward Marcus, who was now able to block every move.

Marcus let out a laugh, reveling in his newfound ability. All the training had paid off. He brought down his sword from beneath and noticed Aedon momentarily losing his footing.

Now is my chance, he thought, and struck hard from the left. Aedon's shimmering blade seemed to gleam as it soared through the air, landing a few feet away.

Marcus had finally disarmed Aedon. He raised his hands in the air and whooped, thrusting his sword upwards. Aedon gave him a curt nod and said, "Well done, boy."

Upon the completion of his training, Marcus was summoned to the grand hall by his father, the King. Marcus made haste to rush to his father's calling. Inside the grand hall, Marcus's father sat upon a throne of gold studded with gems. Beside him sat Marcus's mother on a throne of similar magnificence. A roaring fire crackled in a large hearth adjacent to the thrones.

A coat of arms draped the wall behind them. A bard strummed at a harp in the corner, and the soft sound of music carried throughout the corridor. The ceiling was formed with cedar beams. Against the stone walls, a marble floor stretched across the expanse of the room.

"I hear you have completed your training with Aedon," the king announced with a smile.

"Yes, your majesty," answered Marcus, bowing at the feet of his father.

"Stand, my child, I have a gift for you," ordered the King.

The sound of the hall's doors opening, followed by heavy boot-steps, rang loudly off the walls of the Grand hall. As Marcus stood, he looked back to see Aedon carrying something long and wrapped in green velvet. While kneeling before the King, Aedon stretched out his arms to offer the velvet-covered object to the King. After accepting the object from Aedon, the king motioned for him to stand.

Aedon looked over at Marcus and smiled. It seemed odd because Marcus could not recall ever seeing him smile. But today was different. The King unwrapped the velvet, exposing a silver sword in the shape of a dragon. Marcus gasped when he beheld its beauty.

"Since you are now fifteen years old and have completed your training, I feel it worthy to give you this sword," said the King. "This sword holds great significance and responsibility to this kingdom. This sword once belonged to King Thoren before I struck him down with this very blade while avenging my brother's death, and I want you to have it."

When Marcus took the sword, sunlight shone upon it, casting a magnificent display of colors around the entire room.

"For you to carry this sword comes with great responsibility, and I believe you are ready to care for it," said the King.

"I will be your majesty," Marcus acknowledged, bowing.

Marcus continued to carry that sword on his hip for many years to come. He was always reminded of his duty to the kingdom as he felt the weight of it. Overall, for a sword, it was quite hefty, but in the hands of a wielder, it seemed so balanced that it was practically weightless. He was so honored to be the one wielding it that the next three years were filled with excitement and determination to do his duty well.

But then, Marcus was met with devastating news.

His father and mother had declared war against an army of raiders headed for the castle, requiring the presence of both his parents in battle. Marcus sat in his room and watched as his parents led a large march across the horizon. Unknown to Marcus, this was to be the last time he would ever see them again.

The skies hung low, and rain began to fall. Marcus couldn't help but watch from an opaque window as the view images became distorted by streams of rain falling against the glass. Marcus ran across the room to chase after his parents, but was greeted by a familiar face at his door. It was Aedon. Marcus collapsed into Aedon's arms and began to sob.

For the first time, Aedon embraced Marcus with care instead of aggression. This simple act of kindness warmed Marcus's heart. He now knew Aedon was more than just a teacher. He was a friend. Months passed by and injured or dead soldiers returned, but there was still no update on Marcus's parents or the battle itself. Marcus's heart shattered.

With only Aedon to confide in, Marcus began to lose hope. His heart felt like it was torn apart and scattered to the winds. He was now an orphan. As a teenager still, he was now the King. The burden was too much to bear. Neither food, wine, nor women could soothe his heartache.

That was, of course, until he met Jezebel.

Chapter 3:
Secrets of The Assassin

Aedon was a sheep farmer, and his father Dorian was a butcher. His mother died during childbirth, and his father rarely spoke of her. Dorian was tall, of slender but muscular build for his age. The scar over his eye was well known, but there were others that people had yet to see. Aedon had never told anyone about how he became blind in one eye. His hands were covered in scars from his years as a butcher. He had a burn scar on his neck that he didn't like to talk about. He had a natural scowl on his face that made him feared by most.

Growing up as a butcher's son, Aedon had become desensitized to the sight of blood and death. Many times, Aedon's father would have him accompany him to the butchery. Upon arrival, Aedon could smell the foul stench of rot and decay as slaughtered carcasses were cast into a pile to be hauled off to the woods for the wolves lurking within them. Aedon learned early on not to grow an attachment to living things.

And so Aedon carried a detached demeanor about himself. This learned behavior bled into every aspect of his life. Aedon had always yearned to love and have connections with animals and people, but he struggled to find it in himself to do so. He never really had any friends to play with and always found himself busy either caring for the sheep or assisting his father in harvesting their meat.

Soon enough, Adeon became numb to death. To some, he seemed focused and determined, and to others, he seemed cold and unfeeling. When Aedon came of age, his father allowed him to go to the castle by himself to sell meat. Aedon had his own stand inside the castle walls where he set up and displayed the meat. He always made a fire nearby to keep flies from ruining his chance at making a profit.

All sorts of people would come to the market to buy goods. Aedon would keep a keen eye on the knights and soldiers as they patrolled the castle walls fearlessly. He greatly admired them and their profession. He was determined to be just like them. Without his father knowing, Aedon traded a cut of meat for a two-handed broad sword that was offered as a gift from a knight who had noticed his admiration. Aedon hid the sword from his father's view under a cloth inside the cart, and every time his father would go to the castle alone, leaving Aedon behind, he would brandish the sword and practice with it in the hills overlooking the herd of sheep. The sword was heavy and hard to wield, but as time went on and Aedon continued to practice, the weight of the sword began to feel more and more natural in his hand. Eventually, it seemed to be almost an extension of him.

Aedon knew that his father would never approve of his use of a sword. To Aedon's father, there was enough to kill without ever needing a sword. The boy made sure his father never learned of his new hobby, especially since there was trouble afoot in the village.

Rumors had begun to surface about raiders attacking nearby villages. People spoke of entire villages being burned to the ground and men being slaughtered as the women were either kidnapped or raped. The entire village was on edge because of this news.

One day, while tending to the sheep, Aedon noticed a familiar face riding up the hill towards him frantically. He had often seen the man at the market at the castle. As the man got closer, Aedon saw the sadness in his eyes, and he knew that he had come with grave news. Between pants and gasps, the man told Aedon that raiders had killed his father. As soon as those words came out, Aedon's ears began to ring and his eyes became unfocused. The man went on about how it happened as his father was leaving Glovendall, and that there was no one around to aid the old man as he was attacked brutally. Aedon simply nodded and walked back into his house.

In anguish, for the first time, Aedon found himself totally alone.

His father's body was returned to the farm for a funeral service, escorted by a procession of knights stretching for miles. To Aedon, a simple butcher, it felt excessive. As the horses approached, the earth trembled beneath their thunderous hooves. Banners of the castle rippled in the wind as the solemn march advanced.

At the heart of the procession, a gold-studded carriage bore his father's body, draped in a banner of the castle's crest. The spectacle felt strange, yet Aedon couldn't help but feel honored by the grandeur of his father's final journey. The knights formed a circle around the carriage before dismounting and stepping forward.

Through the long hours of the night into early morning, Aedon had dug his father's grave with his own hands. Now, he watched as the knights carried the body to its final resting place. One of them approached, presenting a sword wrapped in the castle's banner.

Why are they doing this? Aedon thought.

As he accepted the sword, the answer became clear. "For you, Aedon, I present you with your father's sword," declared the knight.

"My father's what? No, I think there has been a mistake," Aedon replied.

"There is no mistake," said the night before, producing a sealed piece of parchment containing the king's wax seal. After unsealing it, the knight began to read it aloud.

"By order of the king of Glaradon, I hereby relinquish the duties of Sir Dorian in fulfillment to the crown upon his final resting place. Having served as a loyal assassin, servant, and friend to the crown for

many years, it is my decree that Sir Dorian be buried with full royal honors and his sword be presented to his only son, Aedon."

"Assassin? What did the king mean by that in his decree?" asked Aedon, confused.

"Your father had spent years as a personal assassin for the king, but had retired after the passing of your mother. May she rest in peace," answered the knight.

As the pieces fell into place, Aedon understood why his father had never wanted him to have a sword. Tears welled in his eyes as a soldier sounded the battle horn, signaling the moment his father would be lowered into the earth.

Needing one last glimpse, Aedon stepped forward and pulled back part of the banner. Beneath it, his father lay clad in full armor and chainmail. *How had he kept this a secret from me for my entire life?* the boy thought. Stunned, he watched as the body descended into the grave.

Then, in a single motion, the sound of a hundred swords being drawn filled the air. A blinding glare of steel rose toward the sky.

"Þar til vér sjá þú again, vér munu fit inn þinn nafn," the knights yelled aloud, which translates to *until we see you again, we will fight in your name.*

Aedon fought back tears. He never knew that his father was an assassin for the king. The thought of the many stories he could be told began to bring a smile to his face. His father was more than a butcher but a hero of the crown.

After the funeral, a knight named Pheldon approached Aedon.

"I have so many questions," Aedon said.

"I can answer any question you may have about your father," Pheldon said, resting his hand on Aedon's shoulder.

"What was he like? You know? As an assassin?" inquired Aedon.

"The best that this kingdom had ever known," answered Pheldon.

"Did you ever fight alongside him?"

"Yes, many times."

"He never seemed like a fighter to me," said Aedon, looking at the floor.

"Never underestimate your father; he was the most vicious killer I ever met," Pheldon corrected.

Never had Aedon imagined that the man he respected, feared, and loved was considered dangerous. At this point, Aedon's mind began to swim with ideas and thoughts about what his father was like as an assassin. Did he dress in all black and sneak around in the middle of the night? Or was he someone who would dress like a local and deliver the final blow to an unsuspecting target?

"How did my father grow into becoming an assassin?" Aedon asked.

"Your father was an orphan who was raised in the castle. When he grew older, he requested the king to allow him to train and become an assassin," said Pheldon.

"If he was an assassin, how did he become killed by a group of raiders?" Inquired Aedon.

"As he fought off his attackers, he was struck by a single arrow," Pheldon answered.

"Did he die alone?" Aedon asked.

"From accounts and reports I received, your father killed 13 raiders single-handedly before being struck down," Pheldon clarified.

As Pheldon, Aedon began to see the hero that his father had been. The thought of this put Aedon's mind at ease and brought a smile to his face. Aedon knew that if he had the chance to avenge his father, he would do so without hesitation.

Aedon continued to raise and slaughter sheep to take meat to the castle in hopes of encountering his father's killer. He was ready and eager to take his revenge. Upon one of his many returns from the castle, Aedon's horse and carriage almost collided with a cloaked figure stepping into the road.

"Ahhh…Please!" came the voice of a woman who was now lying in the road with her hand outstretched.

Bringing the horse and cart to a sliding halt, Aedon stepped down from the cart to assist the woman who had collapsed and become unconscious. He gently pulled back the woman's hood to reveal the face of a mesmerizingly beautiful woman. Aedon was unsure what to do and knew he couldn't leave her where she lay due to the dangers in the area.

Aedon picked the woman up, gently laid her into the cart, and continued home. When he had arrived, he gently carried the woman into his home and set her on his bed. Her cloak was dark green and gold, and her hair was as black as the feathers of a raven. Her lips were full, and her cheek held a slight blush. Her face was slender and encased by her hair.

Aedon sat in a chair across from the woman and admired her as she slept. A subtle groan arose as the woman's eyes began to open. Taking in her surroundings, she found herself confused and bewildered.

"Where am I?" she asked.

"You're at my home. You're safe," Aedon answered as he stood in the corner of the room.

"How did I get here?" The woman asked.

"You fainted in the middle of the road in front of my cart," Aedon stated. "I picked you up and brought you here with me."

The woman attempted to stand, but her knees were weak, and she collapsed onto the bed. Aedon offered her some water, which she graciously accepted. Aedon thought her clumsiness to be adorable. She had a child-like innocence about her that Aedon couldn't help but admire.

"What is your name?" asked Aedon in an attempt to break the silence.

"Devina," replied the woman. "What's your name?"

"My name is Aedon," he answered.

"Where exactly arc we?"

"We are in a little town called Rivenhelm; where are you from?"

"I'm from a town west of here called Glovendall," she said.

Aedon looked into Devina's eyes and found himself absolutely smitten by her beauty. Her eyes were the piercing gray of ice-cold steel. Her eyelashes were thick and dark. Devina had shed her cloak, revealing an entrancing burgundy dress with silver inlay. Her dress was fitted tightly against her hourglass figure. The bodice of her dress encased her bosom. Her dress had long sleeves that came to a point upon the back of her hand. Her hands were smooth and soft. The hem of her dress flowed down into what looked like a pool of burgundy water.

A fluttering nervousness began to fill his chest, and he could feel his heart race. His teeth felt like they were going numb, and a tingle in his jaw began to grow, causing him to stutter. Never before had he imagined that he could have possessed such feelings for another being.

"I-Is there an-anything I c-can get for you?" Aedon began to stammer.

"A chair by a warm fire would suffice right nicely," Devina answered, smiling.

"R-right away," he answered.

Aedon rushed outside and returned carrying three large logs under one arm and a few split logs in the other. Within minutes, Aedon was able to create a roaring fire from the simmering coals that were resting in the fireplace. He retrieved a chair from across the room and placed it close to the fire. Devina took a seat in the chair, and Aedon prepared some food for her. It wasn't much more than smoked meat and bread, but Devina accepted it without hesitation. Aedon pulled up a chair across from Devina and began to ask more questions.

"What were you doing in the woods before I found you?"

"I was running for my life," Devina said in a soft voice.

"From who? Or what shall I ask?" questioned Aedon.

"From a man that I was supposed to be betrothed to," she answered.

"Why did you run?" Aedon asked as he lifted a brow.

"He said he would beat me if I ever refused to bed him before marriage," she informed.

"Have you known him for long?"

"No. I was captured by him and his men when they attacked our village," she said.

"His men?"

"They are raiders, and they go around raping women, killing people, and stealing anything they can while leaving villages burned to the ground," she stated.

"I give you my word that that will never happen again as long as you are here with me. I swear," Aedon reassured.

"Thank you so much for your kindness, but I understand that I must be imposi-" Devina began.

"No, please stay," Aedon begged.

The woman smiled. "Alright, I suppose being in here is far safer than being out there."

A faint sigh of relief escaped Aedon. He found himself both joyful and relieved to hear that she was willing to stay. Something about her made him feel emotions that he had never experienced before. He felt comfortable with this woman, and her elegance seemingly cast a spell upon him.

The sun began to fade behind the trees, and Devina said she was tired. Aedon offered his bed to her and lit a candle on the nightstand beside it. He reassured her that he would be just outside the room if she were to become in need of anything. After a short time, Devina emerged from his bedroom.

"Will you come and lie with me?" she asked.

Aedon was surprised, but this was an opportunity he would never turn down. "As you wish," Aedon answered.

Devina reached for Aedon's hand and escorted him into the bedroom. She climbed into bed and patted the blanket for Aedon to join her. Aedon removed his boots and complied. As he lay back on the bed, he felt Devina's hand on his chest and her head on his shoulder. Looking over at her, Aedon noticed that she was looking into his eyes with admiration.

"Is something wrong?" he asked.

"Yes. Why couldn't I have found someone like you sooner?" she asked. "With you, I feel safe and secure."

Aedon turned to look at the ceiling when he felt Devina kiss him on the cheek. Turning to look at her, he found his lips meeting hers. Instead of pulling away, Devina leaned even closer. Aedon could feel their lips passing over each other and their tongues dancing against one another.

Aedon could taste the flavors of berries and honey on her tongue as they kissed each other. Her hair swelled sweet and reminded him of a fresh melon. As their tongues and lips danced in a lover's waltz, Aedon felt her hand wrap around the back of his neck as she climbed on top of him. Involuntarily, Aedon's hands slid down and rested upon Devina's waist.

Sitting upright, Devina slid down the sleeves of her dress, causing her round, perky breasts to be exposed. She slid her hand over Aedon's and dragged it up to her breasts. Devina then forcefully ripped open Aedon's shirt, revealing his densely toned, muscular torso. She dragged her nails across his chest as she leaned in for another kiss. With a sudden movement, Aedon rolled Devina onto her back, where she began to pull up her dress.

"Take me as your own," she whispered into Aedon's ear.

Aedon buried his face into her hair as he kissed her neck gently while feeling her nails dig deep into the flesh of his back. Devina slid her dress over her head and tossed it on the floor. With her body completely naked, Aedon couldn't help but admire her divine figure.

Her stomach was flat and toned without any signs of ever being pregnant. The curvature of her hips was soft and smooth. Her legs had slight muscular features in her thighs and calves. Her feet were small and flawless.

Aedon began kissing her neck as he ran his hand between her thighs. Devina began to breathe heavily, and her breathing turned into moans. Aedon began running his lips and tongue down her body until he found himself buried between her thighs. The sweet taste of fresh honeysuckle emitted from her flesh as Aedon continued to explore her entire body with his tongue. Her skin smelled of sweet grass and sandalwood. Aedon became completely intoxicated and filled with lust.

Devina raised her legs to her chest as he traced his lips along her legs and his tongue around the protruding flesh between her thighs. It was more than an infatuated feeling that Aedon was experiencing. It was love. For what felt like hours, Aedon explored Devina's body with both his hands and mouth.

Devina forcibly rolled Aedon onto his back and unfastened the tie to his pants. She slid herself on top of him and began to raise and lower herself against Aedon's hips. As Devina continued to rise and fall, Aedon began to release involuntary moans, which became muffled by Devina's kiss.

Aedon began to raise and lower his hips against the rhythm of Devina's motion, causing the blissful feelings they both were having to intensify tenfold. Aedon and Devina found themselves screaming like banshees to the waves of intense pleasure that fueled the ecstasy they felt. With curled feet and clenched fists, they both gave into the crescendo of intense climax.

Devina released a labored exhale and then collapsed upon his chest. Both Aedon and Devina lay on the bed, breathing heavily. Aedon ran his fingers through her hair, and she began to hum with quiet moans of comfort. Unable to speak, both of them lay quietly and took in the sounds of each other's breathing. Soon, Devina drifted into slumber, listening to the beating of Aedon's heart.

The next morning, Devina found herself alone in bed and wondered if she had simply fantasized about the occurrences of the night before. She stepped down from the bed and got dressed to head into the front room of the house, where she found a plate of food and a note. The plate consisted of salted beef with bread, fresh berries, and a glass of wine. The note that was on the table was transcribed as such:

My dearest Devina. Last night was nothing short of pure magic; I am captivated by you and will cherish the moments we share. You have stolen my heart and have given me a smile in exchange. If you need me, I will be on the hill beside the house.

Signed,

Aedon.

The simple words of the note brought a smile to Devina's face. With an overwhelming hunger, she scarfed down the food that was left for her and then folded the note and placed it inside her dress. "*I will keep your words close to my heart,*" Devina thought to herself. She had also grown feelings of love for Aedon. She peered out the window to see Aedon on the hill practicing wielding a sword.

She watched for minutes before she was startled by a knock on the door. When she answered the door, her heart fell to her feet. On the other side of the door stood the man whom she had been running from. The abusive man whom she was to be betrothed to.

Devina tried to shut the door quickly, but the man used his hand and foot to prevent the door from shutting. He laughed manically and threw open the door, sending the girl flying across the small room. The man walked over and grabbed Devina by the arm hard, and forced her to her feet.

"Aedon! Aedon!" she screamed, struggling against the man.

"I hope you've had your fun, but you're coming home with me," the man growled.

"LET GO OF ME! THIS IS MY HOME NOW, AND YOU NEED TO LEAVE!" demanded Devina.

The man slapped her across the face and dragged her outside. The more she screamed, the tighter the man's grip grew. Devina's arm was hurting severely, and tears flowed down her face.

"You will marry me and be a loyal wife by doing as you're told," the man declared.

"I will never love you when my heart belongs to another," said Devina and then spat in the man's face. The man raised his hand to strike her, and she closed her eyes to brace herself. As he brought his hand down on her, he felt the feeling of a large hand grab his arm, preventing him from connecting the blow.

A look of murderous hatred burned in Aedon's eyes as he gazed upon the man who dared to put his hands on a woman. Rage had filled Aedon, and his lack of sympathy fueled this hate.

"Let go of her now. I'm only going to tell you once," Aedon declared.

"Who do you think you are to tell a man how to handle his property?" said the man, releasing Devina's arm and reaching for his sword.

The man brandished his sword with blinding speed and slashed across Aedon's face. Unfazed, Aedon caught the blade in his gloved hand, twisted his wrist, and snapped it in half. He seized the man by the throat and slammed him to the ground, forcing him to drop the broken sword.

Clenching his teeth, Aedon pulled off each glove. With bare hands, he drove his thumbs deep into the man's eyes. Blood pooled around his fingers as each eye ruptured with a sickening pop. The man screamed, thrashing and clawing at Aedon's arms. Aedon pressed harder. Bone cracked beneath his thumbs, and the man fell limp, his body eerily silent.

Aedon had never killed a man before, and he felt no regret about doing it. To him, it was as simple as slaughtering a sheep. He did not have any tolerance for violence against women. Devina did not seem at the least disturbed by Aedon's display of violence.

Aedon stood without so much as a labored breath and wiped splattered blood from his face with his shirt.

"It's finally over; I'm finally free," Devina said, panting.

"I will never let anyone hurt you. I give you my word," said Aedon.

Devina rushed over to throw her arms around Aedon's neck and rewarded him with a kiss of gratitude. Aedon lifted her from the ground with the ease of holding a child and held her in his arms as they entangled each other in a romantic kiss. Aedon lifted the man's body over his shoulder and carried him to the cart. He then hauled his body to a vacant spot in the woods to bury him. Devina accompanied Aedon to make sure that she spat on the man's grave.

Returning home, Aedon carried Devina through the threshold of the door and sat her gently in a chair. He prepared a meal for both of them to celebrate the permanence of Devina's newfound freedom. As they ate, both Aedon and Devina began to talk about their plans for the future.

"I hope seeing that man die didn't disturb you," Aedon stated.

"It didn't disturb me, and yes, I saw it, but I bet he didn't," said Devina savagely.

Aedon was both amused and flabbergasted by her statement, and after a second or two, both of them burst into a fit of laughter.

Within just a few days, Aedon and Devina got married.

The ceremony was extravagant, and the celebrations were spellbinding. Aedon announced his betrothal to Devina while talking to Pheldon one day, and he and Devina rode into the castle to sell meat. With such exciting news, word spread fast.

Now married, Aedon made Devina a promise to avenge her village of the raiders that had caused so much chaos and destruction. He was going to make sure that she was free of their tyranny. He was also going to avenge his father. Shortly after they became married, Aedon devised a plan with Devina to use her as bait to lure the raiders to her so he could kill them. After asking around, Aedon got word that the raiders had set up a camp nearby, and he knew then that the trap was set. Both of them set out to put their plan into action.

Aedon was surprised to find the camp was nearly ten miles away from his home but this fact gave the couple time to prepare.

Aedon and Devina arrived near the campsite and saw see the smoke of their fire rising through the trees. As they inched closer, Aedon saw multiple tents set up in a scattered array. Multiple raiders walked around the campsite as they laughed and talked amongst themselves. Several wooden cages lined the outside edge of the campsite. Inside each cage, multiple women stood trapped like livestock, waiting to either be brutally raped or executed.

The women's cries and pleads for help echoed throughout the forest. Some women were being pulled forcefully from the cages and being dragged into nearby tents to await a session of horrific acts of torture and sexual abuse. Devina had to act quickly for their plan to be successful. Aedon would stand close in case their plan went astray.

Devina walked calmly, with a sense of authority that Aedon found riveting. But he had to remain focused on the plan and not his coitus thinking. As she walked closer, the raiders became aware of her presence. Having been alerted, all the raiders rose to their feet. Now, the plan was in full swing.

"Hey, do y'all remember me?" Devina yelled with slight arrogance.

"I see you have come back to where you belong," said one of the raiders.

"This will never be where I belong. I'm free," she replied.

"GET HER!" yelled one of the raiders.

Devina turned and sprinted toward Aedon as the raiders gave chase, quickly closing the gap. Aedon waited behind a tree, watching Devina run toward him. The moment she darted past, he stepped out with his sword drawn. The raiders, caught off guard, had no choice but to fight.

Before the closest raider could stop, Aedon swung hard, his blade slicing clean through flesh and bone. The raider's torso separated from his legs with a sickening thud, entrails spilling across the ground. Another raider lunged. Aedon sidestepped, hearing the sword whistle past his shoulder. In one fluid motion, he struck, his blade tearing across the raider's face. Blood flooded the man's eyes as he staggered back. Aedon grabbed him by the hair and slammed his head onto a rock. The raider collapsed, face down and motionless. Without hesitation, Aedon drove his sword through the back of the man's skull. As he pulled the blade free, a wet suctioning sound filled the air. Blood pooled over the raider's ears, trickling down on the rocks below.

Aedon scanned his surroundings. He was outnumbered—fifteen to one. Perfect. The raiders circled, blades drawn, like vultures over fresh carrion. He saw fear in their eyes, but they had to die.

With a sudden charge, they attacked. One by one, Aedon cut them down. When the last raider fell, he stood amidst the carnage, blood pooling at his feet. Devina was gone. Around him, bodies lay strewn without pattern—without remorse.

"Devina," Aedon called out.

"Are you looking for this?" said a raider, stepping from behind a tree while holding his sword to Devina's throat. He had her clutched in his arms and she did not more.

"Let her go, and I'll let you live," pleaded Aedon.

"Drop your sword first and kick it away," the raider said.

Devina grunted but did not move, weary of the sharp blade.

"Just don't hurt her," said Aedon.

Aedon complied and threw down his sword. He kicked it aside and raised his hands. Aedon knew that Devina wasn't in any real danger since he towered over the raider and knew a sword wouldn't be necessary to kill him. Aedon wasn't going to let him live.

"You are an experienced swordsman, but without a sword, you are just a man," stated the raider arrogantly.

"Let's settle this then, just me and you," Aedon declared.

"It's settled. I've won, and this woman is now mine to bear my children, so run along before I kill you," said the raider smugly.

This was a mistake for the raider to say. Without hesitation, Devina reached down and clasped her hand around the raider's groin and squeezed as tightly as she could while delivering a swift blow from her elbow to his ribs. The raider dropped his sword. He began choking Devina. In an instant, Aedon had closed the gap between them and grabbed the raider by the throat. The raider's grip around Devina loosened, and he was suspended in the air.

The raider clawed viciously at Aedon's arms and hands as he choked, spit gurgling in his throat. His eyes began to bulge and become bloodshot as his face began to shift to shades of red and burgundy. Aedon released one hand only to grab the raider's leg before bringing the raider back down hard upon his knee with a sickening crunch. The raider's body became limp but was still able to create sounds of anguish. Aedon grabbed the raider by the legs and proceeded to swing his body viciously against a tree repeatedly. After five or six times doing this, the raider fell silent. Aedon grabbed the raider by the torso and impaled his chest on a low-hanging branch. The man was snow dead.

Aedon scanned his body for wounds. He had a long slashing cut on his back and several smaller ones on his arms and chest. His face was dripping blood that was not his own, and his hands had become painted red from his massed slaughter. Blood flowed from the blade of his sword like rain from a leaf during a storm. He was breathing heavily from so much exertion.

The raiders were slain, and the plan for revenge had been executed perfectly.

As the days went by and turned into weeks, Devina began to get sick in the mornings. Aedon was in fear of losing her and tried to accommodate her needs as much as possible.

"My dear, is there anything I can do to better your illness?" asked Aedon.

"Sweetheart, I don't have an illness; I am with child," answered Devina.

For the first time in Aedon's life, he felt pride rising inside him, knowing that he would soon be a father. Devina and Aedon began thinking up a name for their child. Aedon said he had hoped for a strong son who could help him with the selling of meat when he got older. Devina hoped for a girl whom she could raise into an elegant young woman.

Aedon found himself enthralled by the idea of being a father. As the weeks turned into months, Devina began to show signs of her pregnancy. Her belly grew, and her feet had begun to swell. Nearing the end of her pregnancy, Devina fell ill. Aedon continued to remain caring throughout, even when Devina took a turn for the worse. Aedon asked for doctors from the castle to come and care for Devina in her times of medical need.

Medicines and potions were administered, but they had been proven to be ineffective. Devina had grown weak and was unable to walk. Aedon would carry her to the tub and help her bathe. Devina's health continued to plummet. Aedon feared for the well-being of his wife and child.

On a cold night, while the night was clear and the moon was full, Aedon sat at the bedside of his beloved and held her hand as she faded away into death. Aedon felt shattered and completely lost. After Devina's funeral, Aedon found himself searching for ways to end his life because his heart couldn't bear walking this world without the love of his life.

Devastated, he tried poisons that only made him violently ill. He had once tried to hang himself, but the limb of the tree had broken under his immense weight. His final plan was to attack the castle and die at the hands of a knight.

The next morning, Aedon had readied his father's horse and was prepared to die before the sun reached its highest peak. He rode towards the castle as his heart lay broken, and his mind swam with heartfelt memories of his time with Devina. *I'm coming, my love. We will be together soon.* Before arriving at the castle, Aedon was met by a carriage that was under attack by a small group of raiders.

Several soldiers lay dead on the ground after being slain by such brutal savagery. The driver of the carriage was hiding, tucked away under the carriage as the raiders encircled it. The raiders were yelling and calling out in a language Aedon couldn't understand. To Aedon, this was a moment for revenge and a swift death.

Seizing the opportunity to avenge his father's death and to join his wife, Aedon dismounted his horse and withdrew his sword. Aedon charged the nearest raider and swung his sword, splitting the man in half. From his left, he noticed a sword hurling down in his direction. Aedon raised his sword and brought the advancing attack to a halt. With a heavy fist, Aedon punched his attacker in the face, causing him to stumble backward. Aedon then plunged his sword into the chest of his attacker. Ripping the sword away from the man left a large wound emanating from his torso.

Aedon felt another attacker jump upon his back, and with the sound of a loud crunch, Aedon threw his body against a tree, crushing the attacker. After the attacker fell, Aedon raised his sword and drove it through the mouth of his downed assailant. With a twist of his wrist, Aedon freed his sword and swung heavily at the last raider, slicing his head clean from his shoulders.

Aedon realized that he was unscathed from the confrontation, and blood lay strewn everywhere. He couldn't tell whose blood was from where, but the evidence of a vicious slaughter was apparent. Aedon got a sickening feeling of what may lie within the carriage, and before his hand could reach to open it, the door burst open, and a short, fat man stumbled out from inside.

"Thank you so much, mister, for saving our lives from those terrible raiders," said the man graciously.

"It was no trouble to me; I was hoping they would kill me," replied Aedon.

With a look of shock and disbelief, the man stood gawking at Aedon for his words.

"I am the king of Glaradon, and you have saved both me and my infant son Marcus," said the man. "There is no reason that a man of your caliber should be wanting to be killed when you have proven yourself to carry much more use."

"My wife and unborn child have died of a fever, and I have searched for a way to join them across the veil of death," said Aedon.

"Well then, may I at least have the name of the dead man who saved me and my son?" asked the king.

"Aedon, your majesty," he answered.

Aedon had knelt in the presence of the king, offering his sword to the king in hopes that the king would honor his request to die. The king took the sword from Aedon, and instead of unleashing a final blow across Aedon's bowed neck, he dubbed Aedon a knight and protector of the kingdom. Aedon was in utter disbelief.

"As king of Glaradon, I hereby dub thee Sir Aedon. Knight and protector of the kingdom. Now rise, Sir Aedon," declared the king.

"I am honored, but your kindness to me isn't warranted," Aedon stated.

Aedon rose to his feet and accepted his new title. The king offered him a place within the castle since the home he had grown to know was washed in sorrow and heartache. After hard thought, Aedon considered partaking in the king's offer and was given the chance to ride with him and his son in the carriage to the castle. Aedon had never ridden in a carriage before. The inside of the carriage held luxury that Aedon hadn't even dared to dream of.

The seats inside the carriage were made of gold silk and stuffed with wool. A set of satin curtains enshrouded the door and window of the carriage. Hand-carved depictions of horses rested along the top edge of the carriage's inside. The floor was covered by a rug made with elegant patterns and colors. The carriage carried along down the road, and silence filled its air until the king decided to break it.

"Where is your mother or father?" asked the king.

"Dead," Aedon simply answered.

"If I may ask, who was your father?" the king inquired.

"Dorian the butcher," Aedon said.

The king smiled when he heard this. Aedon figured the name of his father would be familiar to him. Knowing now, his father's association with the king came as no surprise to him.

"Glory be! I knew your father, you know? He was my personal protector," announced the king.

"Is there any way I could become an assassin like him?" Aedon asked.

"With a little training, anything is possible," answered the king.

"*I am going to do this for you.*" Aedon thought to himself as the image of his wife entered his mind. The carriage entered the gate of the castle, and the king ordered Aedon to be fitted with armor. Two soldiers escorted Aedon through a doorway on the side of the castle, which led to a series of tunnels and hallways.

After turning corners left and right, Aedon finally arrived at a large wooden door that had been set into the wall. When the door was opened, Aedon found himself standing in what he had perceived to be the armory. Chainmail and armor hung from the walls like metallic tapestries. Swords of various styles sat inside a barrel that rested in the corner.

There was an older gentleman pacing around the room, grabbing tools and tinkering with different pieces of metal. In the middle of the room sat a wooden work-bench that was littered with various tools used in the repairs of metal armor.

"This man needs to be fitted with armor by the order of the king," said one of the escorting soldiers.

"King wants, king wants. Make and fix the armor the precious king flaunts," rambled the older gentleman.

As Aedon stood, the older gentleman began bringing over different pieces of leather and held them against Aedon for measurement. Dashing around the room, the older gentleman began to place some pieces of leather on the workbench while discarding others on the floor. With a wooden mallet and steel punch, the older gentleman began creating small holes in the leather that were later tied together with smaller leather strands.

Piece by piece, the leather articles were assembled and fitted to Aedon's exceptionally large build. Within two hours, the older gentleman assembled the entire torso and sleeves from leather. Aedon wore this and did not feel any added weight placed upon him. The armor, however, took longer to create and form.

After being fitted with armor, Aedon was escorted and given a tour of the castle. The sheer enormousness of the castle was far beyond his wildest dreams. It seemed like every door had a room, and every room held a tunnel. It was a giant labyrinth consisting of rooms, hallways, and tunnels.

The largest room of all was the grand hall where the king and queen sat in their thrones. Aedon was escorted to a large corridor that sat beneath the castle. Stone pillars rose up to meet a large ceiling. Aedon found himself standing in a large corridor.

Scattered throughout the room stood multiple assassins training with weapons against wooden dummies. Some of them had paired together to train in hand-to-hand combat. Aedon was mesmerized by the seclusion of the assassin's training room.

"New killer,' hollered one of the men in the room.

Amongst one of the men, a large man with silver hair walked over to greet him with his hand extended. "I'm Garvon, the instructor here and master assassin. Have you ever killed a man before…"

"Aedon, sir, and yes, I have," Aedon answered ashamedly.

Garvon's face contorted with surprise. Aedon realized the potential consequences of murder.

"How did you kill him? A sword? Dagger? Bow?" Garvon asked with a sinister smile.

"I pressed my thumbs through his eyes until his skull cracked," Aedon said.

At that moment, the room became still, and everyone in the room looked directly at Aedon. Garvons mouth was agape in absolute astonishment. Not a single sound was made, and it became so quiet that Aedon could hear his own heartbeat.

"Good lord, boy, what possessed you to kill a man like that?" Garvon inquired.

"He tried to hurt my wife," answered Aedon with his head hung low.

"Here in this sanctuary, no man has to feel ashamed over taking the life of another man. It's either kill or be killed," Garvon said, patting Aedon's large shoulder.

Aedon was given rigorous training, from hand-to-hand combat to weapons skills. In the beginning, Aedon felt intimidated as he tried desperately to learn each technique as he watched his fellow assassins perform them with ease. After three long and excruciating years, Aedon finally became a masterful, skilled assassin. As a gift from Garvon for his success, Aedon was gifted with a horse that he named Despair. He chose the name so he would always be carried forward from the despair of his past. After his graduation from training, Aedon was called by the king to become a personal guard and protector of the crown.

Chapter 4:
When Angels Wear Crowns

Jezebel was a child who had been thrown into the world as a woman. Her childhood was stripped from her at the age of ten when her village was attacked by raiders. Before this, she was simply the maiden daughter of a weaver. Both her parents were weavers, and they helped to shape Jezebel into the best weaver she could be. Within the village, Jezebel lived next door to her mother's sister, Devina.

Devina was also a weaver. She carried a sense of childlike innocence and wonder when it came to being around Jezebel. On many occasions, Jezebel would visit her aunt, and they would share extravagant tales of make-believe with each other. Jezebel was just like any other child with a rich imagination and active mind.

Jezebel would collect flowers from the bank of a local brook and bring them home for her mother or her aunt to plant and display from the window. There were many instances when she would bring an entire bouquet of flowers to her aunt. At times, Jezebel would catch the occasional butterfly to bring home. She had an eye for beauty in all things, and her charm warmed all of the hearts within the village. She would play outside while her parents worked tirelessly, making fine fabrics that could be sold to travelers and inside the castle.

Jezebel had never been to the castle before, but she loved to hear the fantastic tales told by her father after returning from his adventures. Not only was Jezebel's father able to spin fiber into a yarn, but he could also spin a tale into a magnificent adventure. Jezebel would lie awake at night, staring at the ceiling and daydreaming about the exciting adventures her father recounted.

Her father always surprised her with gifts and trinkets that he came upon while he traveled. Jezebel's family was by no means wealthy, but they never went without. Jezebel's parents would always find a way to provide a warm meal and a cozy place to sleep at night. Her parents had unmatched hospitality and welcomed weary travelers with meals and a place to sleep despite their humble means.

As time went on, Jezebel became friends with some of the travelers' children. They would play outside and create little adventures of their own. Jezebel loved to climb a particular tree near her house with the children and pretend she was a queen, sitting atop a large throne. She ordered the other children to service her bidding.

One of her closest friends was a girl named Agatha. Agatha was a small-built girl with blonde hair and freckles. Jezebel grew to trust her completely. She was not sought after by the boys who would come around. Her clothes were tattered and stained, and her face was always slightly smudged with dirt.

Agatha was feisty, just like Jezebel, and had been known for bloodying a boy's nose once or twice. She was completely unafraid of anything that came her way. Where Jezebel was afraid of snakes and lizards, Agatha would catch them and play with them. She would talk to them as though they could understand her and pretend that all of the creatures that she caught were friends or family.

Because they were like-minded, Jezebel and Agatha found themselves in pretend battles for the power of the throne.

"Who dares to challenge me?" proclaimed Jezebel while holding a large stick – her royal scepter.

"I do," declared Agatha while holding her own stick – a sword.

"Do as you must," said Jezebel while reaching for another stick that was supposed to also be a sword.

Jezebel climbed down from the tree and began to clash sticks together with Agatha in an intense 'sword' fight. They lashed out at each other, dodging blows and attacking viciously. Agatha and Jezebel fought valiantly under the tree while laughing and giggling at each other's poor form. With a gentle tumble to the ground, Agatha found herself defeated and pleaded for Jezebel to spare her life.

"Do you surrender, peasant?" asked Jezebel with a hint of victorious authority.

"I yield, I yield! Spare me, oh gracious queen," Agatha pleaded.

"As your gracious queen, I spare you," Jezebel declared.

Both Jezebel and Agatha fell to the ground in a fit of laughter. Such was their closeness.

They would spend hours lying under the tree, looking up at the sky and watching as the shapes of the clouds went by. Animals – ducks, elephants, lions, and more were called out as they gazed towards the sky. The bond between Jezebel and Agatha seemed unbreakable.

Agatha began to spend the night in the cottage with Jezebel. They would stay awake until late hours in the morning, gossiping about boys and how they were each going to inherit the crown from a handsome prince. The fantasies they shared seemed so unrealistic, but the notion of it was comforting. But their childhood was not all filled with joy.

Word had gotten to Jezebel's family that raiders had been attacking villages along the way to the castle and were recently seen headed south.

Jezebel had grown afraid of the news, but with Agatha at her side, her fears had subsided. Jezebel's parents reassured them that they would all be safe from the raiders and that there was nothing to worry about. If only those words held some form of merit. In two days' time, everything changed.

Jezebel woke up to the screams of villagers running frantically throughout the streets. As she stepped outside the door of her house, Jezebel saw that her nightmares had just come true. Fire and smoke filled the streets as people ran sporadically to and fro. The sounds of their screams and cries filled the air. Jezebel witnessed a black-clad figure run to a pregnant woman, drive a sword through the back of her throat, and then slice open her belly. He allowed the unborn child to fall to the street and then, with a large boot, stomped on it. A splatter of red, purple, and gray stained the ground.

Jezebel screamed in horror and darted inside to find her parents and Agatha. A thick wall of smoke had risen. Jezebel was blinded and called out. Looking up, Jezebel saw flames beginning to lick the rafters of the ceiling, and hot embers rained down on top of her. Not receiving a response, Jezebel ran outside and continued to scream for her parents and Agatha.

That's when she saw Agatha captured by a black-clad raider. Agatha began to kick and claw away at her captor, but he struck her in the face and then stabbed her in the belly. Agatha clutched at her stomach with both hands as blood spilled over her fingers. She gasped for air.

"NO!" screamed Jezebel as she sprinted toward Agatha.

Agatha collapsed to the ground, eyes wide, and looked up at the sky. She tried to speak but was only able to utter unintelligible sounds. Agatha gripped Jezebel's shoulder tightly with a blood-covered hand. Jezebel held Agatha in her arms as she watched the life fade from her eyes and her pupils dilate.

Jezebel's chest hurt, and her stomach throbbed as she began to wail in agony. She heard the sound of two raiders approaching behind her. In the moment of fear, Jezebel felt her body become numb as her adrenaline surged.

In an attempt to flee, Jezebel felt a tightening grip on her arm. Jezebel began to frantically writhe as she tried to break free from her captor. She felt herself being dragged. They pulled her behind a nearby cottage. Then, Jezebel felt herself being flung into a tree, and a bright flash filled her vision.

Jezebel became dazed and weak and felt herself being pushed over and held down upon the back of a vacant cart. Unable to move, Jezebel felt her dress being ripped away, leaving her naked and exposed. She felt the cloth remnants of her ripped dress being stuffed into her mouth to muffle her screams as the raiders took turns violating her and stealing her innocence. At some point, Jezebel felt a heavy thud against the back of her neck, rendering her unconscious.

Jezebel regained consciousness and felt a sharp, throbbing pain from both her posterior and her groin. Fresh blood trickled down the inside of her legs. Struggling to stand, Jezebel began to take in her surroundings. It was early morning, and through the haze of smoke and flames, Jezebel noticed that the raiders had left. Stone husks of cottages stood along the road with windows broken. Mothers, fathers, sisters, brothers, sons, and daughters were seen walking in the destructive aftermath in search of survivors. Dead bodies were laid in a field as mothers wept over them.

Jezebel walked along the ruins of the village naked, searching for her parents. Blood from where she had seen Agatha fall was still present in a blackish-burgundy pool. The image of Agatha, wide-eyed as her life faded in Jezebel's arms, haunted her, but Jezebel had to shake away the memories. Across the road stood a group of surviving villagers examining the remains of those who had been killed in order to identify family members.

Jezebel crossed the road with fears of seeing both of her parents slain in a gruesome display. The bodies had been covered by strands of hay and cloth. Jezebel recognized the hand of Agatha peering from under a cloth. Her blood-stained hand lay lifeless on the grass. The handwoven flowered bracelet that Jezebel made for her was still on her wrist with specks of blood on it. Tears began to flow down Jezebel's face uncontrollably.

Without warning, Jezebel felt arms wrapped around her, causing her to scream before realizing they were the arms of her mother. Behind her stood her father, with tears streaming down his face. Jezebel collapsed into her mother's arms, and her father wrapped a cloth around her to stop her from being exposed. Her father knelt down, and Jezebel threw her arm around him to embrace both of her parents at the same time. Jezebel was too young to understand what had happened to her.

"We are so sorry, Jezebel; we never wanted any of this to happen to you," said both of her parents.

"Where did you go? I couldn't find you, and I saw Agatha and…and," Jezebel began.

"I'm so sorry. I thought you had left with us, and Agatha went back to the house to come get you, but then," her parents began to apologize.

"I saw her, I saw Ag-," Jezebel began before breaking into a fit of tears.

Jezebel's parents did their best to console the distraught Jezebel. Her innocence had been stolen from her, and she wasn't the only one. Upon further inspection, Agatha had undergone the same acts of horror before succumbing to a gruesome death. Jezebel knew Agatha would have wanted to be buried under her favorite tree, and so, she made sure this happened.

Jezebel hand-picked a bouquet of wildflowers and placed them on Agatha's chest. The sound of tears and wailing could be heard throughout the air. Tears flowed from Jezebel's eyes as he watched Agatha's body be lowered to the ground. During her moment of agony, Jezebel has forgotten to see if her aunt Devina is safe.

Jezebel had become frantic once again when her parents had told her that Devina had been taken. Jezebel feared for her as memories of her own horrors ran through her mind. Her memories left her scarred and traumatized. If only there was something she could do. She began to ponder ideas in order to avenge those who had died or had been harmed and how to rescue her aunt.

Weeks had gone by, and there was no word on Devina's whereabouts or wellbeing. Her cottage sat vacant and scarred by the charring of fire that was set to it. Her flowers that had been beautiful at one time had now become burned remnants of beauty. The door to her cottage sat askew, and the wood was singed. What was once full of life and beauty now sat as an empty husk of what had been.

As time passed, Jezebel began to grow more and more defiant of her father and men in general. Her defiance was fueled by the unseen scars that had left her broken and defiled by the raiders. Unfortunately, she wasn't the only one. Most of the women in the village suffered the same trauma as her. Her mother was one of the fortunate ones who got away and didn't have to be subjected to that atrocity.

Her mother had noticed her progressing aggression towards men, from sly comments to full-blown physical attacks. Her father had suffered several instances of these aggressions. Discipline was limited due to the understanding of this behavior. Her parents had to figure out a way to gain control of and assist Jezebel through her trauma.

"Jezzie, we need to talk," said her mother.

"About what, Mom?" replied Jezebel.

"Let's go for a walk, and we will discuss it," suggested her mother.

Jezebel and her mother walked down the road and began to cross a secluded field. Jezebel's mother had asked her why she had been acting so angry towards her father and other men. Jezebel informed her about what the raiders had done to her and how she was constantly reliving the moments that had occurred. She also mentioned that every time she saw a man, the memory would come back as if it were happening again. Jezebel explained how she was constantly being raped over and over due to her trauma of reliving it.

Her mother sat and listened as Jezebel described, in horrific detail, the raping that she had endured. Her mother knew of the rape by the visual blood evidence but had no idea the extent of how brutal it was for her. Her mother had finally come to terms and admitted that she, too, had been raped when she was a little girl by a family member who was later executed for his crimes. She understood the trauma of having to undergo such an atrocity and how difficult it was to live with.

Jezebel and her mother clutched each other in a tight embrace and began to weep over each other's shoulders. Jezebel realized she wasn't alone now that she and her mom had something in common. Just this admission alone sculpted an unbreakable bond between her and her mother. It was an admission that even Jezebel's father was unaware of.

Jezebel began to feel guilty for displaying such unwarranted aggression without any provocation other than having a different physical composition to her. Her mother had suggested she begin making amends with all the multiple men she had displayed aggression towards, starting with her father. Jezebel honestly loved her father and understood that her actions toward him were undeserved. She just needed a way to find an outlet to control her aggression. Her mother suggested weaving as a distraction.

Jezebel began weaving everything from clothes to banners. The distraction from her mind had seemed to be effective in dealing with her trauma. Her days began to fly by her, and her anger had seemed to surface less often. She learned that what had happened to her would stay with her forever. The hours turned to days, and the days turned to weeks, and then she received word of a surprise.

It was midday, and Jezebel had been tirelessly weaving when she heard a joyful commotion outside. She peered outside to see her mother running across the yard in a hurry. Out of curiosity, Jezebel opened the door to peer outside, and that's when she saw it. A horse was carrying a man and woman up the road. The man was unrecognizable to Jezebel, but the woman was, without a doubt, Devina.

Jezebel began to run in pursuit of her mother, who had already recognized Devina sitting on the horse. She and her mother were ecstatic to see her return alive and well. Jezebel began feeling the gaping hole in her heart start to fill. Devina had no idea about Agatha and what had happened to Jezebel the night of the attack. Jezebel could only imagine what had happened to Devina and how similar their stories would be.

Devina was wearing a dark blue dress with white lacing. Her hair had been tied into a neat bun and held together with a blue and silver hairpin. She had on a pair of black boots that protruded beneath her dress as she sat upon the horse.

"Thank goodness you're alive," said Jezebel's mother.

"I owe it all to my husband, Aedon," Devina answered while pointing to the man who accompanied her on the horse.

Aedon dismounted the horse before assisting Devina to the ground. She had been gone for months since the attack and still seemed the same except for a hidden look of depression from the trauma she had experienced before. To Jezebel, Devina was more than an aunt. She was a close and trusted friend. Jezebel and her mother threw their arms around her while giving praises for her return. To Jezebel, Aedon seemed like a man of protection and caution.

Jezebel's father had stepped outside after noticing the rise in commotion. After seeing what Jezebel had endured and how she had responded to it, he found it best that he keep a distance. He had a smile on his face from gratitude that masked his look of caution. When Devina noticed him standing there, she ran up to him and gave him an unexpected hug.

"Aunt Devie, can I talk to you about something?" asked Jezebel while extending her hand to go for a walk.

"Of course, Jezzie," answered Devina.

Devina and Jezebel walked down to the nearby brook, where she and Jezebel discussed the traumas they had both suffered from the attack by the raiders. Jezebel realized that Devina's story of her events was much worse than her own. Not only had she been beaten and raped, but it had happened relentlessly for weeks before she was able to finally escape. Devina informed her about the raider that Aedon killed at his farm. The one who had hunted her down to try to force her to go back to her brutal captors.

Jezebel discussed how she was having difficulty adjusting to her life due to the assault that was inflicted on her.

Devina had advised her that her best approach to handle it would be to share her story among other women who had suffered the same atrocity and lean on one another when times get tough. Jezebel had confided in Devina about how men triggered her memory, and she was constantly reliving the same nightmare while being awake. Devina told her that there were still times when Aedon had to comfort her after waking up and screaming.

Devina also told Jezebel how Aedon had sought revenge against the raiders and slaughtered all of them single-handedly on behalf of all of their victims. This put Jezebel's mind at ease. It made it easier to accept her trauma as a past horrific experience and nothing more. Devina reassured her that whenever she was around and needed someone to talk to, she would be there.

Devina and Jezebel embraced each other in a sympathetic hug before heading back to Jezebel's house. At the house, Aedon is seen having a conversation with Jezebel's parents. Jezebel never felt fear while being around Aedon. Something about him made Jezebel feel safe. Whether or not it was his towering stature or the fact that he had protected Devina from the raiders before single-handedly avenging the entire village was unclear.

After some time had passed, Devina and Aedon departed down the road with smiles and laughter. Jezebel felt more comfortable with men after receiving advice from Devina. Jezebel still remained wary about being around strangers whom she had never met. That part of her would stay with her for the rest of her life.

Years passed by, and Devina continued to visit Jezebel, but her visitation numbers soon decreased. Word had gotten to Jezebel and her family that Devina had grown ill. Jezebel began to grow a sickening feeling of loss since it was Devina whom she had relied on for so many years to help her cope with their traumas. If anything were to happen to Devina, she would become totally lost and hopeless. Jezebel began to plead to any entity that would listen to keep Devina alive because she felt as though she couldn't live without her.

Winter had come with a ferocity, and the frigid cold set into the air. For days, snow fell, and the wind howled like the screams of wolves. The cold air had pierced through everything inside and out, making the fireplace nearly useless. Jezebel and her family had begun to hang thick furs across the windows and doors in an attempt to keep the frigid cold at bay. The raging winds whipped across the cottages, forcing snow drifts to pile along their sides and nearly burying the doors underneath.

When the snowstorms had settled, a thick blanket of frozen wilderness was all that remained in view. Within the snow, chimneys billowed plumes of smoke in an attempt to fight against the winter's brutality. The stables nearby were nearly buried in snow, and the chilling cries of horses could be heard. Villagers had made their way outside to witness the aftermath of the brutal frozen storms that had passed.

Many of the villagers had made their way to the stables only to find a heart-wrenching sight - horses dead after succumbing to the immense cold. Her heart was shattered, and the loss was devastating. From down the road, a single rider on horseback approached the village. The rider stopped in front of Jezebel's parents and handed them a rolled piece of parchment.

This grew Jezebel's curiosity, but she soon realized she was not ready for the purpose of the encounter. Jezebel watched her mother's face as she read the inscription on the parchment, which caused tears to fill her eyes. Jezebel's heart sank at the possibility of what the parchment read. Jezebel reached for the note in order to read why her mother seemed so distressed.

"I'm so sorry, Jezzie," her mother apologized while choking back tears.

Jezebel began to read the note that was written and quickly understood why her mother had begun crying. The note read:

Jezebel's heart was completely shattered now after receiving word of her aunt's passing. She felt hopeless for her future, and the world around her began to spin violently until she had lost consciousness. Jezebel's parents rushed to her aid after witnessing her collapse and carried her inside. Even though she was unconscious, Jezebel held firmly to the note in her hand.

Jezebel was beyond devastated. As she opened her eyes and the room around her came into view, the realization of the news came rushing back to her. Jezebel sat clutching the note as tears streamed down her face. She found herself in absolute disbelief.

Her mother and father tried as hard as they could to console her. Jezebel found herself feeling emotionally exposed, but her parents reassured her that they would always be there when she needed them.

"I'm so sorry, Jezzie," said her mother.

"What am I supposed to do now?" Jezebel cried.

"We have to live for her and keep her memory alive," her mother answered.

Jezebel contemplated the idea of death out of fear of not being able to face the world. Devina was the only one in her life who made her feel as though she had the strength to overcome any obstacle. Now that Devina was gone, those feelings had faded away. Jezebel climbed to her feet and stepped outside to let the chill of the wind hit her face. It wasn't calming to her but instead a reminder to her that she was alive.

With a deep breath, Jezebel swore to herself that from that day forward, she would live her life the way she believed would make Devina proud. She understood that she had to find the strength within herself to take on the world in Devina's absence as she had done before. She could hear Devina's voice in her mind, giving her words of encouragement. The thought of hearing those words from her made Jezebel smile and gave her a sense of security.

Weeks passed, and the snow had finally melted, leaving the roads washed in mud. Jezebel had grown a strong connection to her parents since hearing about her aunt's passing. She had learned to become a successful weaver and made some of the most elaborate fabrics and clothes the village had ever seen. She learned to make extravagant patterns within the fabric that she had woven.

Jezebel's parents would attempt to invite her on journeys to sell the woven goods that they had made, and she would always politely decline. She felt safer in the village, where she was familiar with her surroundings. Even though the village had been horrifically attacked in the past, it was the only place that she felt she could call home. Every day, Jezebel would walk down to the brook and pick fresh flowers to place on Agatha's grave, and they would exchange the ones from the day before. Many times, she would sit at Agatha's graveside and have conversations to motivate herself to face the day.

Agatha's grave was the only place where Jezebel could express her feelings and share her secrets. Many of the secrets she would reveal were secrets that she kept from everyone, including her parents. She would talk about her fears and the hope of being able to fall in love with a boy someday. Never did she imagine the future that awaited her.

Many years had passed, and Jezebel grew older. She was eighteen years of age and had officially become a woman. She had found herself desired by many men within the village and travelers from afar. Even as efforts were made, Jezebel continued to deny their advances. Her view towards men had changed since she was a child, but her caution had not changed. Jezebel and her family had become quite lucrative amongst the others within the village. It was by no means the revenue of nobility but instead sustainable to their needs.

Jezebel had become gracious within the village, and her family assisted others in times of need. For years since the attack, people in the village no longer had to go without. Any evidence of the attack had been long gone since the village was rebuilt. Families prospered, and children learned from a young age how to weave fabrics like their parents did. The community had become unified and leaned on one another to grow towards a promising future.

During a fall evening, when the leaves had changed color, Jezebel noticed a small caravan advancing from the road. The convoy was lined by horses and banners from the kingdom of Glaradon. Jezebel lost her impression of the kingdom after the attack on her village, which left families without aid. Not a single correspondence to assist them had come from the castle, and this had a sour taste in her mouth. She hoped that none of them would stop and just continue passing through.

This was not the case, and Jezebel seemed both disappointed and annoyed. In the center of the caravan, a gold lace carriage with a team of six white horses could be seen. The carriage had exquisite carvings of lions and wolves. There were also intricate carvings of flowers that traced the doors and windows. A brass handle was fitted to the side of the door, and a small velvet step hung underneath. Jezebel found the carriage to be majestic and bizarre at the same time.

A soldier on horseback sounded a horn before another soldier dismounted to open the carriage door. When the door swung open, Jezebel glimpsed the inside, lavishly adorned with red velvet and golden accents. It far exceeded anything she had ever encountered in her life. A young man, no older than Jezebel, stepped out of the carriage.

His clothing hinted at nobility, and he carried himself with the poise of royalty. Jezebel realized he was too young to be the king, so she guessed he must be the king's son. His hair shone as bright as fresh hay, and his eyes sparkled in a stunning shade of blue. The garments he wore seemed crafted by the finest weavers and seamstresses in the world, and Jezebel imagined she would never possess such skill.

The young man's tunic displayed a deep blue with gray accents, and he draped a gray and black cloak lined with white fur around his shoulders. Around his neck, he wore a silver necklace studded with sapphires and black diamonds. His trousers matched the gray of a stormy sky and met white stockings and black boots.

His full lips and fair skin enhanced his striking appearance, and his piercing gaze made Jezebel's heart flutter. She fought her emotional attraction, not wanting to appear obvious in front of a stranger. To mask her feelings of deep desire, she decided to adopt a smug and off-putting demeanor, hoping it would keep him from noticing her. When their eyes finally locked, little did she know he felt the same way about her, and he would soon become the man she would marry.

Chapter 5:
Hope for a New Dawn

Upon approaching the castle, Jezebel grew uneasy, noticing the things around her. She could hear the sounds of children at play and smell the scents of fried food. Everyone within the castle had a purpose. Some were harvesting grain while others crushed it into a meal. Pigs lay in muck inside their pens. Jezebel saw a man carving a sheep for meat behind a store.

As hammers rang out, striking against anvils, Jezebel felt overwhelmed by her emotions. The carriage rolled through the castle gates, and a choir of trumpets filled the air.

When the carriage came to a stop, Aedon opened the door. With an outstretched hand, Aedon helped Jezebel to her feet. She was escorted inside by Marcus. As Jezebel and Marcus made their way into the castle, Marcus was greeted with bows from the servants roaming the halls. At the end of one of the many halls in the castle stood a large wooden door. Marcus opened the door, revealing a room fit for the highest royalty.

A four-poster bed draped in red silk sat against a wall. An array of fir blankets and velveted pillows covered the bed. At the foot of the bed, across the room, was a large hearth with a roaring fire. Flowers hung along the walls and littered the bed. A mirror sat at a desk with an assortment of perfumes bottled in various shapes, sizes, and colors.

A bear-skin rug was laid on the floor in front of the hearth. A chair sat in front of the desk, from which hung a beautiful green and blue dress. A silver necklace with a topaz pendant was laid across the dress.

"This is all for you, my dear," said Marcus.

Jezebel stood speechless, admiring her surroundings.

"Anything else I can get you?" Marcus asked.

"If I am to make you a banner, I will need a loom, fiber, and dyes," answered Jezebel.

With a nod from Marcus, two servants bowed and raced down the hall. Within an hour or so, the servants returned with a loom and a chest full of fibers. A satchel of bottled dyes was draped over the shoulder of one of the servants.

Jezebel found herself alone. She was supposed to work on her given task. She teased each fiber into thread and meticulously dyed each one a variety of colors. Working tirelessly, Jezebel finally finished the banner shortly after nightfall.

With a gentle knock at the door, Marcus entered to check Jezebel's progress. "How far have you gotten on the-" Marcus' mouth hung open in shock.

Before him, draped over the bed, was a banner more exquisite than Marcus could have possibly imagined. The banner was checkered in black and red and featured the family crest embroidered in its center. The crest depicted the head of a stag with antlers made of arrows and crossed swords beneath it. A line of flowers trailed along both sides of the crest.

Both the top and bottom of the banner were layered in silver fringe. Each square contained a yellow fleur-de-lis. Marcus was in complete amazement at the banner.

"Do you like it, your highness?" Jezebel asked coyly.

"My dear, I am absolutely smitten by it," said Marcus.

Marcus dashed across the room to embrace Jezebel.

"I shall hang it from the castle landing at first light," Marcus continued.

"Stay with me tonight," requested Jezebel.

"Stay with me forever," replied Marcus.

"I wish to marry you, Your Highness," Jezebel stated.

"Then you shall have it," whispered Marcus.

"Our love will no longer be clandestine," continued Marcus.

Brushing the banner to the floor, Marcus and Jezebel climbed on top of the bed and became tangled in passion. They writhed amongst the fur, passions unfurled to blissful ecstasy. With bodies drenched in sweat and breathing labored, Marcus and Jezebel found themselves ensnared by captive emotions they both displayed for each other.

As the fire burned down to embers in the hearth, both Marcus and Jezebel watched as the burning timber fell asunder. Jezebel began to drift into a slumber, but her dreams were not of bliss. Instead, they consisted of a horrific nightmare. In Jezebel's dream, she awakened to the widow opening and a cold draft entering the room to snuff the embers within the hearth.

Jezebel stood too close to the window but could feel herself levitate from the floor.

"Come to me," said a male voice, but he sounded distant and detached.

Jezebel tried to form words to awaken Marcus, but no sound could be made. Jezebel's body rose above the ledge of the window and was carried out into the nightscape.

"Come to me," Jezebel heard calling.

The air was cold against her skin as Jezebel drifted into the forest. In the darkness, she could see herself being carried to a distant clearing where moonlight pierced the surrounding fog.

"Come to me," called the voice in the fog.

Jezebel saw the figure of a man sitting on a fallen tree.

"No, no, no," pleaded Jezebel. *It can't be him,* she thought.

As she neared and the fog began to lift, Jezebel confirmed that the figure was the same figure that had haunted her dreams. A few feet away, Jezebel descended upon the forest floor. The soil beneath her feet felt cold and damp. Jezebel pulled her gown tightly around her to shield herself from the chilling winds. After Jezebel had visual clarity, the figure before her was indeed Corvainius.

Jezebel's heart raced, and her vision began to pulse. She wanted to run but could not get her legs to move. Corvainius stood and approached her. The stench of decay and damp earth was becoming nauseating. Corvainius placed a hand on Jezebel's belly. "I shall have you both," Corvainius stated.

"Wha-" said Jezebel before she found herself being hurled backward.

Jezebel clinched her eyes closed as the winds ripped past her. She screamed and opened her eyes only to find herself sitting upright in her bed beside Marcus. She leaped from the bed, shaking in fear. Marcus leaped to his feet in a sudden burst of terror.

"What is it, my love?" asked Marcus in a panic.

"It was him again," said Jezebel, her voice shaking, her fingers clawing at her face.

"It was only a dream," Marcus reassured.

"If it was just a dream, explain why my gown is torn, and soil is in our bed," exclaimed Jezebel.

The commotion alerted a guard close by and prompted him to burst into the room with a sword drawn.

"Is everything alright, your highness?" inquired the guard.

"Do me a favor and have the number of guards on watch tonight doubled," Marcus ordered.

"Right away, your Highness," answered the guard before racing down the hall.

"Do you believe me now?" Jezebel questioned.

"I do believe you have sent me into a fright," answered Marcus.

"Why don't you believe me?" asked Jezebel frantically.

"Shh, my love, I never said I didn't believe you. I merely do not know how to explain it," said Marcus, holding Jezebel in his arms.

Jezebel began to calm down with the comforting embrace. After placing a kiss upon her forehead, Marcus stepped over and closed the window. He then called for a servant to reignite the fire in the hearth. Once the fire was lit again, Marcus asked Aedon to stand watch over Jezebel while he tended to the arrangements for the unveiling of the banner Jezebel had woven. Before Marcus left the room, Jezebel called to him.

"Your Royal Highness, there is something I must confess," said Jezebel.

"Yes, my love?"

"I am with child," answered Jezebel.

"Blessed be this day," announced Marcus with glee.

Marcus ran and lifted Jezebel into the air while spinning her around the room. Marcus could not have been more proud.

"I will begin making arrangements for us to marry," declared Marcus with joy.

***

The sun had begun to rise over the mountains beyond the castle, and the talk of the royal wedding buzzed about the halls. Marcus opened the door of Jezebel's room and relieved Aedon of his watch.

"Are you ready, my love?" asked Marcus with his hand extended.

"Yes, Your Highness," answered Jezebel.

Before him, Jezebel stood in majestic beauty only possessed by angels captured on canvas. Jezebel shone brightly in the rays of sunlight that flooded through the window. The silver necklace with a topaz pendant glistened between her bosom. The green silk of her gown was sealed around her divine figure. From her waist, folds of emerald green silk fell to the floor.

Waves of auburn hair fell upon her shoulders. Jezebel's lips looked as soft as the petals of a fresh rose. A faint blush lay upon her cheeks. Jezebel accepted Marcus's hand and was escorted through the halls with Aedon behind them carrying the banner. Marcus led Jezebel to a set of spiraling stone steps. At the top of their ascent was a large wooden door and a guard.

The guard opened the door, exposing a landing outside that overlooked a crowd of people below.

"All my loyal subjects," Marcus announced.

"I have searched far and wide to find hope. Here before you lies the hope that we have all desperately desired," Marcus continued.

Aedon stepped to the ledge, unveiled the banner, and tied it to it. The crowd below erupted in cheering and applause, and the air changed to one of uplifting joy instead of sorrow and desperation.

"I have another announcement," Marcus called aloud.

"I am to be wedded this afternoon to this divine beauty, Jezebel of Glovendall," continued Marcus.

Again, there was another eruption of cheering and applause. Jezebel and Marcus descended the stairs into the castle, where a servant met Jezebel.

"Come, my dear, we have a wedding to prepare for," said the servant.

As Jezebel entered her room, a flurry of servants hurried to and fro. A beautiful white dress lay on the bed, while a pair of silver shoes rested on the floor. Jezebel experienced a crushing tightness as a corset was fastened around her. The dress was then lowered over her torso, and around her waist, she wore a belt adorned with silver trinkets and gems of diamonds and moonstone.

Jezebel wore a silver crown atop her veil. Aedon accompanied her to the grand hall, which was draped in glorious splendor. White and silver ribbons danced across the ceiling, and wedding banners hung from the walls.

An archway of birchwood stood in front of the thrones that sat in the back of the room. The hearth was capped with white roses and carnations. As Jezebel approached the archway, the sounds of a wedding march filled the air. At the archway stood Marcus, as handsome as ever. Marcus was wearing a silver and white tunic and white trousers with boots and a silver clasp. On his tunic, Marcus wore a single white rose upon his chest.

The locals from around the kingdom stood in rows as Jezebel ascended the steps to the archway, and the music faded. Marcus was visibly nervous, and his chest began to quiver. Between them stood a priest to unite them. Both Jezebel and Marcus seemed too nervous even to speak.

After announcing their vows to one another, Marcus raised the veil over Jezebel's face and stood in awe. He was amazed by the simple notion of spending the rest of his life with this mesmerizing woman.

"Your royal highness, you may now kiss the bride," announced the priest.

With gentle grace, Marcus leaned in to kiss his bride. A burst of excitement and celebration filled the hall. A standing ovation from the crowd greeted the newlyweds. Marcus and Jezebel went to their room to consummate their marriage. They clutched in a lover's embrace, and Jezebel's dress fell to the floor. She slid upon the fur blankets draping the bed.

She lay split-thighed with her arms set behind her. Marcus removed his trousers and tunic and joined Jezebel on the bed. As Marcus's clothing fell to the floor, his hands glided along Jezebel's legs. He began to kiss her body, moving upwards from her ankles. As Marcus advanced his kisses across Jezebel's hips, she reclined upon the bed. Her body began to quiver as Marcus caressed his hands along her thighs. Kissing across Jezebel's stomach, Marcus used his hands to tease the jaunty flesh between her thighs.

Jezebel began breathing heavily as waves of erotic pleasure passed across her entire body like an ocean current crashing against a rocky shore. Marcus led his kisses to Jezebel's lips, muffling her moans. Jezebel guided her hand along Marcus's waist and began to stroke his swollen phallus. Both Marcus and Jezebel began to quiver and convulse in ecstasy.

Marcus's voice began to flutter with every movement of Jezebel's hand. With her other hand, Jezebel began to run her fingers through Marcus's hair and clutching tufts every time he dragged his lips along her neck. Marcus wrapped his arms around Jezebel's porcelain-like thighs and pressed himself deep into her.

While Marcus held his arms under Jezebel's thighs, Jezebel wrapped her legs around the small of Marcus's back and used her legs to assist the motion of Marcus's hips. Jezebel had a fluttering feeling passing through her entire body with every thrust. She began to bite her lip to muffle her screams of elation. When both Marcus and Jezebel reached the climax, a surge of euphoria passed over both of them.

"Your royal highness," said Marcus through labored breath and a smile.

"Your Royal Highness," Jezebel repeated.

Condensation began to sweat from the walls due to the exertion of their passion. Marcus spoke as both of them collapsed onto the bed, staring at the ceiling.

"You have made me the happiest man to have ever lived," said Marcus.

Jezebel rolled over on top of Marcus's chest.

"I shall be the proudest wife this world has ever known," Jezebel declared.

Marcus and Jezebel lay naked on the bed and watched the silhouettes of their bodies dance on the walls by the light of the fire. The days flew by quickly. After what had seemed like only mere moments, nine months had passed by. Each day was filled with a new adventure, and the flames of their erotic passion seared each night.

Over time, Jezebel's belly had grown significantly alongside the love that she and Marcus shared. Jezebel suffered at the beginning of her pregnancy due to nausea and an insatiable hunger, but Marcus was always there by her side to hold back her hair and ensure her cravings were met. One summer morning, Marcus awoke early to tend to diplomatic arrangements. Soon after, Jezebel leaped from her sleep in panic, calling loudly for Marcus.

Jezebel's screams for Marcus could be heard clearly throughout the entire castle. Running in terror, Marcus burst through the door with a frantic look of concern on his face.

"What's wrong, my dear? What is it?" Marcus panicked.

With a smile, Jezebel looked at her feet as she stood in a puddle of fluid.

"It's time," said Jezebel while wincing in pain.

Marcus ordered Aedon to fetch the midwife immediately. Without hesitation, Aedon dashed down the hall with blistering speed. Servants began to enter and exit the room, bringing linen and basins of water. Marcus laid Jezebel down on the bed and waited for the midwife. Servants came by and dabbed a damp sponge across Jezebel's forehead. Both Marcus and Jezebel let out a sigh of relief upon seeing the midwife.

The midwife casually walked to the foot of the bed and proceeded to raise Jezebel's sleeping gown. She was given a series of instructions as to how to place her legs and when to push. Holding tightly to Marcus's hand, Jezebel began to push with every bit of force that she could muster. Jezebel's screams of agony carried loudly throughout the castle. With every push, sje could feel a piercing pain as if her body was being torn apart from the inside. After one final push, she gave birth to a beautiful, healthy girl. Jezebel collapsed from the sheer pain and exhaustion she had endured.

"I want her name to be Natheilia," said Jezebel through exhausted breathing.

"I like that, and she is perfect, just like her mother," replied Marcus.

Chapter 6:
From Bitter Ends Come New Beginnings

From a young age, I was a child filled with imagination and wonder. I would always find myself in trouble doing things I was not supposed to do. I once climbed up a tree only to hurl myself into a pond while I was on an outing with my parents. I was always frightening them, attempting what others wouldn't dare.

I learned a lesson that carried me throughout my life. To know when enough was enough. But to me, it was never enough, and I continued to yearn for more. The more difficult, the better. I was always up for a challenge. Being told it was enough always pushed me to greater difficulties. To me, claiming something was enough was like a bird standing on a precipice and never trying to fly.

"One of these days," my mother would always tell me.

We would later sit and laugh at the thought of my fearless antics. I knew I was never in any real danger since my father was recently crowned king before I was even born. My father's closest friend, Aedon, was always in charge of my well-being. But it wasn't going to be easy for him, and I was determined to see that it was so.

With him, I was very defiant and onerous. With every chance I had, I would slip away from view and hide around the castle. Aedon would become frantic in his search for me, and I would begin to laugh, which would ultimately lead to my capture.

"There you are, Nathelia," Aedon would say through a sigh of relief.

"You found me," I would say with glee while finding myself in a fit of laughter.

Years went by, and I saw my mother less and less. When I did see her, she looked feeble and pale. To me, my mother was still the most beautiful woman I had ever known. I loved how her auburn hair accented the slender shape of her face. Her eyes were a frosty gray with hints of gold.

My mother's lips were full, and she always carried a smile when I saw her. Every chance I had to see her, she greeted me with hugs and kisses. Her hugs always felt warm and comforting, and her kisses could cure any ailment I could possibly have.

I would spend time with her, playing with my dolls, or she would tell me fantastic stories about how she and my father met. I loved hearing the stories she told and the adventures that filled them. Sometimes, I would pretend to be the characters of her stories, or I would use my toys and play make-believe with them to be puppets to depict the characters.

Sometimes, I would curl up next to my mother and be lulled to sleep by the sound of her humming and the feeling of her rocking me back and forth. A couple of times, I was gifted with a song that she had learned when she was just a little girl. Her voice was that of an angel's, and to this day, I still haven't heard a voice that could compare.

As the days passed, I noticed that my mother would have fits of coughing to the point where her face became red and her eyes bloodshot. I had no idea this was an early sign of her illness, and she always played it off so well.

Shortly after I turned five years old, I was summoned to my mother's room. Holding Aedon's hand, I was escorted through the castle, where I saw servants lining the walls crying.

"Why are they all so sad?" I asked Aedon.

"You need to see your mother," Aedon replied while dodging the question.

I saw a tear beginning to fall on Aedon's cheek, which was briskly wiped away by his gloved hand. Sorrow had filled the castle, but I didn't know why. As I entered my mother's room, servants were gathered around my mother's bed. Beside my mother, I saw my father kneeling and holding my mother's hand. When my father turned towards me, I could see his eyes were puffy and tear-filled. I saw my mother lying in bed, drenched in sweat.

She seemed faint, but to me, she was still beautiful. My father motioned for me to come closer.

"Why is everyone so sad?" I whispered to my father.

"Your mother is very sick, my dear," my father answered, choking back tears.

"Your mother needs you more than ever right now,' he continued.

My father lifted me and sat me on the bed beside my mother. Her face was flushed and pale, but her eyes were still shining and beautiful.

"Nathelia," my mother struggled to whisper.

"Momma, what's going on?" I asked.

My mother began to cough droplets of crimson onto a handkerchief. Her entire body convulsed with every breath.

"I love you more than anything. You know that right?" said my mother through labored breath.

"Yes, momma, I do," I replied.

I was holding a handmade rabbit doll with buttons for eyes. I offered it to my mother.

"Maybe this will make you feel better," I said sympathetically.

"Thank you, my dear. I pray that you never lose your compassion and innocence," my mother answered.

I threw myself upon my mother and wrapped my arms around her. My father ordered the room to be cleared, and I didn't want to leave.

"Take her away from here. She doesn't need to witness this," my father told Aedon.

Aedon wrapped his arms around me and pulled me away. I could see my mother's outstretched hand reaching for me, but it was out of my grasp. As Aedon carried me out of the room and into the hall, I saw a man enter the room, but nobody else seemed to notice. As the man walked past, time stood still. For a moment, the air felt cold and damp.

The man was wearing aged clothing that was covered in stains. His skin was pale, and he reeked of death. Without turning his head, he briefly glanced at me from the corner of his eye. When our eyes met, my heart stopped. I couldn't breathe. The man disappeared into my mother's room as Aedon carried me under his arm.

It was as if nobody could see the man except for me. I had never seen this man before and wondered if it was a friend of my father's, so I didn't question it. The image of his face would be etched into my mind for the rest of my life. The sheer presence of this man made me afraid and confused at the same time. After some time had passed, I could hear my father shouting across the castle.

"Help, help! She's gone," my father yelled.

Without hesitation, Aedon dashed away, leaving me alone in the grand hall. I started to chase him as fast as my little legs could carry me. Down the hall, servants were gathering around the door to my mother's room, murmuring amongst themselves. As I pushed my way into the room, I could see that my father was in a state of hysteria. I noticed that the window was open, and my mother was nowhere to be seen.

"Where is she? Where is my wife?" my father yelled while viciously shaking a servant.

"I don't know," pleaded the servant before rushing out of the room in terror of my father.

Pacing frantically around the room, my father stopped and placed his hands on the window ledge with his head bowed.

"I want every inch of this damned castle torn apart and searched," ordered my father through gritted teeth.

The guards stood in fear and hesitation, terrified of my father's rage.

"GO!" yelled my father.

Within seconds, the room was deserted of all except my father and me.

"Papa, what is going on?" I asked.

"My dear, I need you to go to the grand hall until I return for you," said my father in a caring but concerned tone.

"Where is Momma?" I asked.

"Just go to the grand hall, and I will find her," said my father.

A servant escorted me to the grand hall. As I waited, I began to hear whispers of conversations I didn't understand. Two servants stood against the wall, talking in secret. Now and then, one of them would glance towards me, and I began to feel uneasy. When my father finally returned, night began to fall upon the kingdom.

"Did you find her? Did you find Momma?" I asked in angst.

"No, my dear, not yet, but we will," assured my father.

I wrapped my arms tightly around my father, and tears flowed from my eyes uncontrollably. My father allowed me to sleep in my mother's room that night at my request. I lay awake most of the night, wondering who the mysterious man was. I couldn't shake the unsettling feeling that began to overwhelm me. Aedon stood in the room with me at the request of my father.

"Who was that man who came in with my mother earlier?" I asked Aedon.

"What man?" asked Aedon with peaked curiosity.

"The man I saw entering the room as we were leaving," I answered.

"You saw a man entering here when we were leaving?" asked Aedon with uncertainty.

"Yes," I clarified.

"Do you remember what he looked like?" Aedon inquired.

"Yes, I can't seem to get the image of him out of my head," I stated.

"Come with me, child," said Aedon, reaching for my hand.

Climbing from the bed onto the floor, Aedon grabbed my hand and escorted me to my father's room down the hall. Aedon entered the room and had me wait in the hallway outside while he spoke to my father. Within moments, the door to my father's room burst open, and my father stood there with a look of concern on his face.

"Am I in trouble, Father?" I asked.

"No, not at all," said my father, kneeling before me.

"Can you tell me what the man that you saw looked like?" my father continued.

I nodded yes, and he picked me up and carried me into the grand hall. Sitting in my father's lap and surrounded by guards, I gave the most detailed description that I could. After I gave my testimony, my father waved his hand, and I was escorted into the hallway by one of the castle's servants. A heavy conversation broke the silence from within the grand hall.

"What are we to do, Your Majesty?" said a guard.

"She has seen his face and may be in grave danger," another guard stated.

"Make her my ward, your majesty," Aedon spoke.

Ward? What did that mean? Was I going somewhere? After a pause, I heard my father speak.

"Fine then, it is settled. Sir Aedon, I hear by, grant you governorship over my daughter, Nathelia," said my father.

"You will take her to Blynehorn at first light, and she shall stay there until instructed otherwise," he continued.

"Understood, Your Majesty," acknowledged Aedon.

The doors of the grand hall opened, and guards began to fill the halls. My father and Aedon were the last to leave the grand hall. My father knelt before me and informed me that I was to go with Aedon at first light. When the sun began to rise, I saw a servant carrying a satchel of my belongings and placing them in a cart that was pulled by a team of horses. My father escorted me to a carriage, where I saw Aedon sitting atop a white horse in the front of the convoy.

Aedon's horse was beautiful. The barding of his horse looked like the scales and wings of a dragon. The breastplate was black leather and inlaid with rubies. There were steel coverings over the hooves. Aedon's saddle was black and silver with a solitary ruby on the horn. The stirrups were inlaid with silver and rubies.

He had to be one of the most elegant-looking stallions I had ever seen. The horse's name was Despair. We set out for the long journey to Blynehorn. My heart sank as we passed under the gates, leaving the castle. I sighed heavily, leaned against the door of the carriage, and just stared out of the window. I began to ask myself questions: *Am I going to see mother and father again? Will I ever return to the castle? Where is my mother? Why won't she talk to me?*

I had never been to Blynehorn, and as much as I loved adventure, I was overwhelmed by sadness. I had never traveled without both my parents. If I hadn't had the reassurance of Aedon with me, I would have been crippled in terror. The winding gravel road we traveled felt as if it had been magically carved through the landscape. We traveled over high hills and through deep valleys.

Through the window of the carriage, I could see that we were coming upon a thick forest with trees reaching up and touching the heavens. I was mesmerized by their magnificent size. I looked towards the top of them, and they seemed to be going forever. I felt like I was trying to peer through the forest to see as far as I could. All I could see were trees until I saw something that made my heart stop.

Behind a tree in the distance, I saw a man standing, but he vanished from view as another tree came between us. It was the same man I had seen before leaving my mother's room. With it only being a fleeting glance, I started to doubt my senses. Was it real? Or was it merely a memory I wished to be real? I shook off the feeling and continued to focus on the journey ahead.

Chapter 7:
A Demon Walks Amongst Us

Corvainius lived in a small town called Castoria. It was full of people who possessed different skills and trades. The town seemed cozy to outsiders and traders alike, but the reality was that it was a town full of struggling craftsmen and farmers. People made things from toys to liquor and from weapons to furniture. Castoria had it all and then some as far as the needs of weary travelers and recent homesteaders were concerned, but trade had been slow due to its lack of travelers. It wasn't because it was not a cheerful place, but because it was hidden from the knowledge of most people. Those who would find themselves in Castoria were merely there by accident.

At the age of sixteen, Corvainius had only just begun his career as a carpenter. Under the apprenticeship of the town's master builder, Mathius, Corvainius developed skills and honed his woodworking ability. With a hammer and chisel, he learned that anything could be crafted from wood, and his imagination was limitless.

Despite his noble ambitions, Corvainius' father was just a struggling farmer burdened by heavy fees and dues imposed by the crown, leading the family to often go hungry. Much of Corvainius' clothing came from scraps of fabric found on the roadside.

Corvainius' mother was a small store owner who sold baked goods and grains traded by travelers and locals. She was a humble woman with the ambition of becoming a royal baker for the king and queen. Each day, she would share her dreams of preparing lavish feasts for the royal court and attending extravagant parties. Occasionally, she would find herself waltzing with an unseen figure while humming songs.

The house that Corvainius lived in was a three-room shack on the edge of town, where they lived mostly in isolation. The front door of the house always hung, a reminder of a particularly violent night of his father's drunkenness. The windows were drafty and cracked. The entrance inside the house displayed poverty at its lowest level. The wooden beam floors were gapped and broken in places. The walls were made of handmade brick that had started cracking in many areas. The ceiling was made from large oak beams that were laid by a team of twelve men.

In the center of the room sat a rickety table covered in flour and melted candles. The table had only one chair, which Corvainius' father occupied, along with two stools and a log serving as additional seats. A handmade chair stuffed with straw and covered in an array of fabric pieces rested in the corner. To the right of the room was a small stone fireplace featuring an iron cauldron. Above the fireplace hung a wooden plaque displaying two swords.

To the left side of the room stood a metal tub, concealed by a long strand of various bathing cloths. In front of the tub lay a hand-woven rug. In the corner of the room sat a wooden chest filled with linen scraps.

In the rear of the room stood a hallway leading to two bedrooms with plank wood doors covering the entrances. Corvainius' room was nothing spectacular. Inside his room was a bed made from straw and a blanket made from pelts of various animals. A single desk made by Corvainius sat at the far end of the room, opposite the bed. A melted-down candle made from cow fat sat in the center of the desk. Corvainius would sit here to pray to any entity to save him and his sister from the turmoil of their father.

His sister Cordelia's room was slightly different from his in that a small bureau sat against the wall across from her bed, and a similar desk was at the end of the room. The desk was also crafted by

Corvainius to match his at his sister's request. A dress made of various fabrics and a pelts cloak draped over the bed. An array of flowers sat in a wooden makeshift vase that her mother had gifted to her, positioned by the window. The window had broken panes and was stuffed with straw to block out the bitter winds of winter nights.

Corvainius' parents' room was much more pleasant than his and his sister's room. A large four-poster bed sat against the wall at the room's center. An assortment of fur pelts draped the wool-stuffed mattress. A fireplace was set into the wall at the side of the room. A desk and cracked mirror sat adjacent to the bed. Multiple handmade brushes made of birchwood and horsehair sat atop the desk. A wooden carving of the family crest hung on the wall above the bed. A window of glass stained by berries cast a variety of colors into the room. Open timber beams lined the ceilings of every room in the house.

Outside, animals ran loose around the yard. Pigs, goats, and chickens wandered as they pleased. A single horse sat in a wooden pen underneath a lean-to connected to the hay loft. Geese and ducks would swim and play in the pond beside a tree across from the house. Wildflowers grew along the walkway to the house's entrance. A long dirt path traveled away from the house and led into town, and the stones hidden within the soil had been worn smooth by the traveling of carts, horses, and rain.

Corvainius loved his parents and his work, but the one thing he cherished above all was his younger sister, Cordelia. Nothing could part them as they were always together everywhere. Many boys fancied Cordelia as she began to mature into a young woman. She had lustrous gray eyes and soft features. Her lips were full and vibrant. Her hair was auburn, and her skin was soft and fair.

She was of a slender build, and signs of womanhood were approaching early. Boys would try their best to win her over, but

Cordelia always rejected their advances. Cordelia did have an interest in boys, but she did not want to be seen astray by her strict upbringing and lack of her father's approval.

As Corvainius tirelessly shaped and built things from wood, Cordelia would always drop by just to surprise him and get a glimpse of the newest project that he was assigned to complete. Cordelia wanted so much to be like her older brother, but was always told it was men's work and that she needed to learn her place. Her father once found her hiding in a hayloft, whittling wood with a knife in order to imitate her brother.

For that action, her father had her struck seven times with a leather strop. When Corvainious received word of this, his temper raged, and he struck his father repeatedly with a piece of wood that left him in a coma for weeks. Upon emerging from a coma, Corvainius' father alienated him and refused to speak to him ever again. After the incident between Corvainius and his father, Cordelia never again received so much as a raised hand from their father. Corvainius regretted not killing his father that day and hated the man that he was.

Corvainius' father carried a problem that he perceived could be fixed at the bottom of a bottle. Night after night, both Cordelia and Corvainius would lie awake listening to the sounds of their mother screaming from being struck while their father was in a drunken rage. When this happens, Corvainius will have Cordelia climb out the window and hide inside the hayloft. When his mother's beatings would cease, Corvainius would see the door to his room burst open and find himself having to fight for his life against his father.

Many times during this, Corvainius was knocked unconscious by an unseen fist delivered from his father. When he would awaken, he would find his father passed out drunk on the floor. Oh, how many times he could have ended the terror there and then, but out of respect for his mother, he let sleeping dogs lie. He then rushed out to the hay loft to ensure that his sister was safe. "Cordie, are you here?" Corvainius called out.

"Over here," Cordelia would reply with a rustling from a pile of hay.

"Are you alright?" he asked.

"Yes, I'm fine. What about father? Is he still angry?" she asked.

"Don't worry. Father won't be bothering us for a while," he reassured.

"Oh my goodness, look at your face," she said.

Up to this point, Corvainius hadn't thought to look at himself, instead focusing on his sister's well-being. Corvainius gazed into a bucket of water and saw the reflection of his face. A large bruise had begun to form on the side of his face from where his father had struck him. He also felt the painful swelling on his head where he had fallen unconscious. Dried blood crusted from the corner of his mouth.

Corvainius dipped his hand into the bucket to not only wash away the blood from his face but also to disfigure his reflection from view. Anger filled Corvainius as he watched the crystal clear water become red in hue from the diluted droplets of blood. As a young man, Corvainius thought of himself as a protector of his sister and swore to her that he would never let their father hurt them again.

Corvainius took up an apprenticeship as a carpenter to ease his parents' financial burdens. His father detested him for lacking the financial success that his son displayed. Whether or not his father saw himself as a failure to provide like Corvainius, one thing was for sure: He would never win his father's approval.

From early mornings to late nights, Corvainius was tested on his craftsmanship by his mentor. He would have Corvainius craft entire pieces of furniture from solid logs, and he never complained. The most tiring part of the craft was when his mentor would have him go out to harvest wood.

His mentor would take Corvainius into the woods on a horse-drawn cart and have him cut down trees with an ax.

"More wood Corvainius! More wood!" Mathias would yell.

Did the mentor ever assist in the cuttings? No. He would sit on the cart and bark orders at Corvainius. Even with his hand sore and his back hurting, Corvainius continued to work. His hands would crack and bleed from the intense labor of felling trees and chopping them into pieces that would fit into the cart.

The hours were long, and the pay was feeble at best, but it was something that helped the family fight starvation. Once, Corvainius had crafted a magnificent chair for his father, and the next day, he found it sitting outside of a market. His father sold it for a bottle of rye. Corvainius found himself crushed and defeated and wanted to find some way to get away.

Corvainius worked as an apprentice for nearly three years until he was promoted to becoming a master builder. With his newfound promotion, Corvanius could now travel to the castle with hopes of selling goods that he crafted. That night, a fight broke out between him and his father.

"What is wrong with you, Father? Why can't you just be happy for me just once?" Corvainius yelled.

"Do you think that somehow you're better than me with your job? Snapped his father.

"Yes, actually I do! I provide this family with more than a belly full of rye and a beating every night," Corvainius snapped back.

With a staggered movement, Corvainius' father pulled back his fist and made a feeble attempt at a punch. But with Corvainius sober and much faster, the punch was deflected. Corvainius' father lunged at him, and they both crashed to the floor. Rolling around and exchanging blows caused Corvainius' mother and sister to become quite frightened. Furniture was overturned or broken in the struggle for dominance between father and son.

"STOP IT! STOP IT RIGHT NOW, YOU TWO!" Corvainius' mother screamed.

Rolling beside the fireplace, Corvinius' father grabbed a handful of soot and hurled it into Corvainius' eyes. While unable to see, Corvainius' father threw sucker punches and cheap shots at him. Unable to defend himself, Corvanius curled up into a ball on the floor while his father wreaked havoc upon his body.

After exhausting himself completely, his father finally walked away and collapsed on the floor. Corvainius dared not move until he heard the all-too-familiar thud of his father. He struggled to move, his ribs bruised and a finger broken. Corvainius began searching for his sister and mother to inform them that he was leaving and didn't know when he would be back. He went to his room to pack a satchel of belongings when his sister burst in, tears streaming down her face.

"Take me with you. I beg you," Cordelia pleaded.

"I have to leave. It isn't safe for me here anymore," he said.

"Please," begged Cordelia.

"You have to stay here and keep Mom safe from the likes of him," said Corvainius while nodding towards the hallway.

"Let me go with you. I'm afraid he will hurt me again," she pleaded.

Cordelia tried to grab hold of Corvainius' arm to stop him, but he was too strong and pulled himself away. He was determined to leave, and as much as he would miss his sister, he had to do what he thought was best for himself and the family. As the miles grew between Corvainius and his home, his resentment towards his father never faltered. He had to focus on getting to the shop to pick up goods and proceed to carry them to the castle. The idea of going to the castle excited him, but the idea of being so far apart from his sister began to break his heart.

As Corvainius walked to the shop at the edge of town, he took a moment to take in his surroundings: the endless rows of trees that outlined his neighbors' fields. His neighbor was standing outside, waving with a grateful smile. Every time Corvainius walked past, they would give each other the same greetings.

"Hello, Corvainius," said the neighbor.

"Hello, Mr. Killgorne," Corvainius would say in reply.

"Headed into town, are we?" Mr. Killgorne asked.

"Yes, sir, I have to pick up goods and furniture, and I will be headed to the castle to sell them," Corvainius answered.

"If I may ask, what did you do to your hand?" Mr. Kilgorne asked.

"Oh, you know, been working with wood," Corvainius lied.

"Will you be gone long?" inquired Mr. Killgorne.

"Perhaps a couple of weeks, and then I shall return," said Corvainius.

"I shall keep a watchful eye over your family in your absence," Mr Killgorne stated.

"That will be much appreciated," Corvaius replied.

With a friendly nod and a wave, Corvainius continued on his journey to the shop. Mile after mile had passed, and the sun had begun to fade over the horizon. Night had set upon the town by the time Corvainius arrived. He loaded what goods he had to sell and hitched the horse to it. The shop was generic but also full of things that would bring wonder and awe to the eyes of children.

Furniture and wooden toys lined the inside of the shop. The roof of the shop was thatched, and its walls were made from stones bought from a river close by, laid by hand, and secured together with sand and mud mortar. The floor was made from timber that had been hewn by hand and laid in rows. A workbench with a mixture of hand tools and wooden mallets on it sat against the wall at the rear of the room. Wood shavings littered the floor around it. A large pile of shavings sat next to a makeshift clay fireplace and was used for kindling.

Corvainius retrieved tables, chairs, toys, and other goods that he believed would sell well at the castle. The cart was handmade with horizontal wooden spindles lining its sides. Wooden pegs locked the wood into place. After securing all that he wanted to bring, Corvainius began the long journey to the castle.

It had seemed that the miles were endless, and the night felt eerie. Corvainius remained focused and driven as he crossed the treacherous miles to the castle. He found himself traveling through thick woods or into roaring waters. The moon that night had only offered him limited visibility of his surroundings. The road to the castle was rocky and full of dangerously large indentations created by previous travelers and torrential rains.

Tall silhouettes of trees reached skyward and seemed to vanish among the clouds above. The cart creaked and groaned as the journey continued. For most, the sound of a moving cart would fade into the background, overshadowed by the beauty of the scenery. However, at night, the noise became nearly deafening as it traveled down the road. The sounds echoed throughout the landscape with an unsettling reverberation in the air.

With every mile passed and every obstacle crossed, Corvainius felt a sense of relief knowing that he was gaining distance from his father. The night seemed calming to him, and the journey allowed him time to let his mind wander. He began to think of his sister and envision her in his mind. He began to replay memories that he shared with her, remembering the wonderful times they had together. He also began to envision that his trip would gain him enough wealth that his family would never want for anything again. Even his father, as much as he hated him.

Before long, what had seemed to be only minutes turned out to be hours. Corvainius had reached the edge of the forest and could see the castle in the distance. The sun had begun to rise over the horizon, casting an orange glow along the side of the castle as Corvainius watched.

Within a couple of hours, Corvainius had finally reached the entrance to the castle. He took in the smells of the air and caught hints of smoke and fresh meats. He could also smell the scents of fresh loaves of bread and baked goods. Corvainius found himself entranced by all of the wonderful scents.

Inside the castle courtyard stood several freestanding markets that sold a variety of goods. People drifted from one market to another, browsing the newest goods of the day. Corvainius had never seen so many people since he lived in a small town on the edge of the kingdom.

Corvainius walked through the markets looking for a place to sell his goods. A small clearing towards the middle of the courtyard sat vacant, and Corvainius found it to be a suitable location to display his goods. After assembling a display for his goods,

Corvainius began to ask around in search of sleeping quarters in the area. He was informed of an inn that sat at the bottom of the hill in a small town called Darvainia. When the sun had set, Corvainius decided to retire for the night and threw a large canvas over the remaining goods he hadn't sold that day.

Corvainius detached his cart from his horse and rode through the gates into Darvainia. The town seemed mysterious after dark. Most of its shops were closed for the night, and very few people were out and about. Riding through the town, Corvainius finally found a wooden sign hanging that said Darvainia Inn.

Corvainius dismounted his horse and hitched it to a post outside the inn. He proceeded inside and was greeted by the innkeeper. The innkeeper was a short, fat man with a thick goatee and partial balding. His hair was thin on his head, but the hair on his arms was thick and dark. He wore an apron that made Corvainius think of a bartender.

"How can I help you, son?" said the innkeeper.

"I am in search of boarding," Corvainius answered.

"How long will you be with us?" the innkeeper inquired.

"I should be gone in less than a fortnight," Corvainius responded.

After paying the Innkeeper for his room, Corvainius ventured out in search of food. Finding something to eat in a town that seemed nearly deserted at night proved itself to be difficult, but with luck, Corvanius finally prevailed. Entering the pub, Corvainius asked for food to eat and was also given ale, which he had never experienced before. The taste was bitter and unappealing to him, but he continued to drink it gratefully. As he drank and ate, Corvainius began to feel a difference in himself that he did not recognize.

His body felt lighter than usual, but he wasn't levitating, and the room seemed as though his vision began to play in slow motion. The feeling was new but enjoyable. The more he drank, the more the feeling intensified. Corvainius attempted to stand but was unable to feel his legs. He nearly fell to the floor before catching himself on a nearby table.

The floor felt like it was beginning to sway side to side, and Corvainius had developed tunnel vision. He found that it was increasingly difficult to formulate clear sentences as he tried to communicate with people. Drowsiness had set over Corvainius, and he found it difficult to keep his balance while walking. He felt like every step was on a suspended piece of string. Corvainius stumbled his way back to the inn and found his quarters. He then crashed onto the bed and faded out of consciousness.

Corvainius awakened the next morning to a searing pain as daylight streamed through the window. His head pounded with every sound, no matter how faint. Corvainius realized that what had happened the night before was his first experience of becoming drunk. He gained a greater understanding of the experience, but wondered why anyone would choose to do that to themselves. Especially his father, who did it every day and night.

Corvainius lay in bed until the excruciating pain that throbbed in his head subsided. When Corvainius was finally able to emerge from the confines of his room, nearly half of the day had been wasted. He found himself having to rush back to the castle in hopes of being able to make a daily profit. Arriving at the castle, he saw that his cart and belongings were still covered from the night before.

Corvainius had several visitors come by to browse or purchase some of his goods. Children running around the courtyard would stop to admire the toys he had made. They would dash off but later return with a parent to buy the toy they had so desperately wanted.

Only a few hours had passed since Corvainius' arrival at the castle that day when a disturbance at the gate caught his attention. A man was standing at the gate, waving and shouting in a panic. It was his neighbor, Mr. Killgorne.

"Corvainius, Corvainius!" shouted Mr. Killgorne as the guards of the gate blocked his entry with spears.

"Let him through. I know him," shouted Corvainius to the guards.

Mr. Kilmore looked exhausted, but Corvainius could tell by the look on his face that something was wrong. The guards stepped aside, and Mr. Kilmore galloped his horse into the courtyard in front of Corvainius. He was drenched in sweat, and he had heavy bags under his eyes. Corvainius could tell by his appearance that he had ridden hard through the night to see him, and it had to be something urgent.

"What is it? What's wrong?" asked Corvainius.

"It's your sister. Your father has murdered her," answered Mr. Kilmore frantically.

"What? How?" asked Corvainius as a guilt-wrenching sickness came over him from the news he had just received.

"Last night, I rode by your farm, and I heard shouting. That's when I saw your father beating your sister mercilessly before he…he," Mr. Kilgorne answered before he was choked up by tears.

"He what?" I need to know," said Corvainius as his sorrow began to form an unrelenting rage inside of him.

"He grabbed her and broke her neck like a twig. That's when she went limp, and I could tell she was dead," Mr. Kilgorne continued.

"Was there anything with my mother? Was she harmed?" Corvainius inquired.

"No. After your sister was killed, I saw your mother run outside, and when she saw what had happened to your sister, she jumped on a horse and fled," Mr. Kilgorne answered.

"Where is my father now?" Corvainius demanded.

"The last I saw of him, he was headed to your barn," Mr. Kilgorne answered.

"I hope he's there when I arrive," stated Corvainius.

"What are you going to do?" inquired Mr. Kilgorne.

"I'm going to kill him," answered Corvainius through gritted teeth.

Without another word, Corvainius leaped onto his horse and bolted out of the gate, leaving his cards and all his belongings behind. He couldn't care less about them at that moment because he was blinded by rage and hatred. Corvainius started imagining various scenarios for how he would plan to kill his father. For years, he had contemplated taking his father's life but never committed to it due to his mother's request. But now that his mother was gone, nothing stood in his way of fulfilling his dark desire.

Corvainius had been running on pure adrenaline, and as it began to wear off, he found himself becoming fatigued. He decided to set up camp in the forest off the road, which was only a day's ride from avenging his sister. *"Enjoy your life while you can because it's going to end soon,"* Corvainius thought to himself.

Corvanius had started a fire when he heard the sound of a carriage and horse approaching from a distance. The creaking wheels echoed throughout the forest like a loose drum. As the cart drew nearer, Corvanius noticed a man perched on the front of the carriage, guiding a single horse along the road through the trees. The man slowed his horse as he approached Corvanius and asked if he could join him. Although Corvanius considered telling the man no, he decided against it, thinking he could use the company.

"What brings you into this part of the forest?" asked the man.

"I stopped to set up camp for the night," replied Corvainius.

"Where are you headed, kid?" the man interrogated.

"I'm headed home to avenge the death of my sister, who died at our father's hand," answered Corvainius fearlessly.

"I can help you with that if you would allow me to show you," the man interjected.

"How do you think that you could help me?" asked Corvainius sarcastically.

"Follow me to my carriage, and I will show you," the man demanded.

Corvainius followed the stranger to his cart, where the man opened the door to his carriage and stepped inside, motioning for Corvainius to follow. Inside the carriage, Corvainius saw that the walls were lined with various bottles of different sizes and colors. The stranger reached out and grabbed one of the many bottles off the wall, handing it to Corvainius. The bottle contained a red liquid that seemed to almost glow in the moonlight.

"What is this? Poison? If so, I don't need it. I have other means of achieving my revenge," clarified Corvainius.

"Consider this a gift," answered the stranger.

"What does it do?" inquired Corvanius.

"It will give you the power to flawlessly seek the revenge you desire and will make it impossible to die while bringing back the one who becomes avenged," stated the man.

Without so much as another syllable, Corvainius tore off the lid of the bottle and drank its contents. The taste was bitter and sweet at the same time. Corvainius felt his stomach begin to cramp with a ferocity that was undeniably the worst pain he had ever experienced. He felt the walls around him begin to spin, and his vision became blurry. He found it hard to breathe, and his head began to feel like it was going to rupture from his shoulders. Corvainius was afraid that he had been poisoned. Reaching out to grab hold of anything to keep him upright, Corvainius collapsed, and everything turned black.

With the feeling of having drowned and taking his first breath, Corvainius came to and began gasping the air around him. The pain in his stomach had partially lessened, but was still quite noticeable, and his mouth grew an immense pain. Corvainius fought to bring himself to his feet. Outraged with his condition, he didn't know how he was supposed to be stronger when he was in absolutely no shape to fight.

"What have you done to me?" demanded Corvainius.

"I have given you the elixir to allow you the revenge you so desperately seek," answered the man.

"Why am I feeling this pain in my mouth and stomach?" Corvainius asked while holding his hand across his stomach and pressing his other hand to his mouth.

"Let me fix that for you," said the man, brandishing a dagger and turning himself away.

After a few seconds, the man turned around and offered Corvainius a wooden chalice containing a thick red liquid.

Something about the smell of it was too enticing for him to refuse. Without a second thought, Corvainius downed the contents of the chalice. As the contents entered his body, Corvainius felt a warm fire pass through his body. Instantly, Corvaninius was able to sense the results of the elixirs that he had consumed.

The world around him seemed brighter and more vibrant. His visual distance, along with his other senses, had enhanced dramatically. He felt entirely stronger. His body felt lighter yet more resilient. He was able to pick up sounds in the forest that he would never have heard before. He could hear the rapid breathing of animals from far away. Looking at his horse, he noticed something different.

He could see every vein in its body shining like golden threads on a red tapestry. He could see each strand of veins pulsating within the body of the horse, and he found himself entranced by this. As he watched this, a hunger pain began to rise in his stomach. The man had noticed his difference, but when Corvainius looked at the man, he could not see any golden strands on his body.

"Now, this gift comes at a cost," said the man.

"For this, I am willing to pay anything it takes," said Corvainius, embracing the feeling of his new senses.

"In order to bring back your sister, your first kill must be the one by whose hand she had fallen," the man stated.

"Oh, I plan on it," reassured Corvainius.

"But in order to keep your sister alive, you must consume the essence of human life every day. A life for a life," declared the man. "The essence?" asked Corvainius.

"Yes, the one thing humans can't live without. Blood," the man answered.

"Can I only drink the blood of humans?" asked Corvainius.

"No, but only the blood of humans will keep your sister alive, but if you need to indulge, you can consume the blood of animals also," the man clarified.

"What happens if I feed on my sister by accident?" Corvainius inquired.

"You can not pass your gift to her, and if you feed on her, she will die," stated the man.

"Pass the gift to someone? Explain," demanded Corvainius.

"You can pass the gift to anyone, but in order to do so, you must feed on them, and when they are at the cusp of death, you must feed them blood from yourself," the man informed.

"Anything else I must know?" asked Corvainius.

"If you don't feed for a day, your sister will die, and it will be permanent," the man warned.

Corvainius stepped outside the carriage and took a deep breath, inhaling the night air. A sudden urge to run overwhelmed him, and in an instant, his feet carried him at blinding speed through the forest. Corvainius could see in the dark with the same clarity as if it were daylight. The night cast a bluish hue around him as he peered into the darkness.

Corvainius had realized he had crossed a great distance without any sign of fatigue. He came to a sliding stop and attempted to leap into the air. To his amazement, he noticed himself ascending high above the trees and was able to see across the vast landscape. Corvainius descended back to the ground quickly, and without any effort, he was able to catch his fall gracefully upon hitting the ground.

Running through the forest to return to the mysterious man, Corvainius noticed that the carriage and the man had vanished as if they had never existed. Corvainius remembered that he was once on a mission to avenge his sister's death and decided to run the rest of the way, leaving his horse behind. What would have taken him a day to ride, Corvainius was able to cross the distance in only a few minutes.

Corvainius had stopped at the entrance of his family's farm and began using his newfound senses to search the property for his father. His vision had shifted from a bluish hue to a deep red. Corvainius's rage started to rise. He could smell the scents of his father's liquor and sweat wafting from the barn. Corvainius walked toward the barn, where he found his father sitting on a piece of wood beneath the hayloft in the center of the barn. After a few moments of Corvainius standing at the entrance of the barn, his father finally noticed him.

"What are you looking at, you ungrateful fool?" His father drunkenly barked.

"You know what you did, and you are going to die for it," answered Corvainius.

Corvainius' father jumped to his feet, nearly stumbling, and reached for an axe sitting nearby. Corvainius was too enraged to even begin feeling any sense of fear. He was able to see the same golden strands that covered his father's body, which stirred an uncontrollable hunger within him.

"Come and take your best shot, you despicable excuse for a son. Yeah, I killed your sister. And I knew it would bring you back so I could kill you too," stated Corvainius' father.

Corvainius' father raised the ax in an attempt to swing it, and as if it had moved in slow motion, Corvainius grabbed it, stopping the blade from doing him any harm. He grabbed the ax and threw it aside so hard that it broke through the side of the barn. Without any sense of control and giving into the feeling of unbearable hunger,

Corvainius instinctively grabbed his father and drove his teeth as deep as he could into his father's neck. Blood rushed through each puncture and filled his mouth with a taste so sweet it was almost like a drug, and Corvainius had to have more. At this moment, Corvainius was unable to hear his father's screams of pain through the feelings of euphoria.

As the intoxicating taste of blood filled Corvainius' mouth, he began to turn his head side to side to further increase the lacerations in his father's neck, causing his blood to rush from his body at a greater volume. Corvainius could no longer hear his father's screams, but instead, the receding pulse of his father's heartbeat. As his father's heart stopped, the earth began to shake violently around him.

Corvainius dropped his father's lifeless body, and then the shaking stopped. A distant but familiar call for Corvainius rang out from outside the barn, prompting him to rush out to find its source. Between the house and the barn, Corvainius discovered his sister sitting upright, emerging from a mound of dirt that surrounded her. He could see the golden strands within her body but resisted any urge to give in.

He rushed to his sister and assisted her up from what was once her grave. She seemed confused and horrified at the same time, wondering how she was alive when she remembered their father ending her life after feeling a sharp crack in her neck. Corvainius informed her that their father was no longer going to hurt either of them and told her about how he had changed in order to bring her back.

He told her what the man had said about how Corvainius had to feed on the blood of humans every day, or else she would be dead permanently. Corvainius was struck by disbelief to hear his own sister say that she would be ok with him killing every day in order to keep her alive. Corvainius escorted his Cordelia inside the house and left her there while he went off to dispose of his father's body.

Corvainius still felt disgust for his father as he looked upon his lifeless corpse. Spitting on his father's body, Corvainius only threw a small amount of dirt onto him, leaving parts of him exposed to the elements. "*The animals can have you*," Corvainius thought to himself. The relief he felt rushed over him and made him release a sigh of gratification.

Corvainius realized just how powerful he had become, and it felt exhilarating. His speed and hearing increased very noticeably. His vision and smell had multiplied tenfold. He thought to himself how incredible an adversary to mankind he had become, and he was finally able to protect his sister without fear for her safety. The hours seemed to stand still, and Corvainius took advantage of them.

Entering the house, Corvainius found his sister sitting alone and staring into the embers of the fireplace. Corvainius stood in disbelief in the doorway of the room, thinking hard about what had transpired that day. He had not come to terms with it all yet. His sister had been dead and buried, and now she was alive and well.

"Are you alright?" asked Corvainius while showing concern.

"How did this happen? How am I alive?" Cordelia asked, confused.

"In order for you to live, our father had to die. A life for a life," answered Corvainius.

"Am I like you? A creature of the night?" questioned Cordelia.

"No, you are just as human as you have always been, but I am left with this curse in order to keep you alive," he clarified.

"Can you make me like you?" she asked.

"No, sadly, since I am responsible for keeping you alive, if I tried, you would die permanently, and there would be no way to bring you back," he answered.

"How will you do this?" she inquired.

"I will have to walk this earth in this state until the day you grow old and die," Corvainius answered.

"Then we shall grow old together without the painful torment of our father," she said.

Corvainius stepped outside to clean the blood from his father when he noticed the sky had begun to lighten and morning was going to be upon them soon. He took a pail of water and washed away the pool of blood that had been spilled on the ground, and, with his boot, he covered over any traces with hay.

The sun had started to cast an orange glow on the roof of the house, creeping down its side toward the barn. Corvainius felt exhausted and wanted to retire after such a long, suspenseful night. When he stepped into the sunlight, his body began to burn and smoke, and his hand caught fire, causing him to let out a painful scream.

As he reeled backward into the barn, the burning ceased, and his body began to heal instantly. His clothes were singed, and smoke was still rolling off the fabric. Having heard the screams, Cordelia rushed outside to the barn only to find Corvainius covered in smoke. Fanning violently, Cordelia found Corvainius unharmed, but there were charred marks on his clothes.

"What the hell did you do?" she asked frantically.

"I don't know. I started to walk inside, and I began to catch fire," Corvainius answered, confused.

"Is it from the sunlight?' asked Cordelia in an attempt to find answers for the mysterious occurrence.

"I don't know, but we can find out," he answered, unsure.

Corainius approached the edge of the barn with caution and slowly extended his hand into the sunlight. Instant searing pain and smoke began to emit from it. Pulling his hand back quickly, they discovered the answer to their question.

"What are we to do now?" asked Cordelia.

"Leave me be for now, and when the sun goes down, I will be able to join you," declared Corvainius.

"Wherever you are, I want to be. Wait here," she instructed.

Cordelia ran inside the house and returned with two fur blankets. She climbed the ladder of the hay loft and extended the offer for Corvainius to join. With a single bound, Corvainius ascended the height of the hay loft and settled down beside Cordelia. She was completely amazed by this, and the expression on her face said just as much. Cordelia and Corvainius fell into slumber in the darkest corner of the hay loft, and when they had awakened, the sun had already fallen behind the horizon, and the moon had risen in its place.

Corvainius felt hungry, and so did Cordelia. He had to leave his sister behind to find an unexpected victim to satisfy his cravings. Upon his return, his sister offered him food that she had prepared, but the thought of eating it disgusted him. Only one thing appeared more appetizing than the food he had grown accustomed to eating.

Corvainius still carried no guilt with him, knowing he had killed two people, one of whom was innocent. Every morning, Cordelia and Corvainius would retreat to the hayloft and emerge only when the sun had set. They would sometimes go into town at night, where Cordelia would become envious of the clothing or jewelry worn by some women who also roamed the night. She would ask Corvainius to procure the items she desired by having him kill those women and steal their possessions.

Corvainius would always loot jewelry and money from his victims, viewing them as no longer needed. He and his sister had amassed a substantial amount of wealth within a few months, and Cordelia had built up an impressive collection of fine jewelry and elegant gowns. Neither of them felt shame for their greed and often flaunted it in public.

This went on for months, and Corvainius became careless about disposing of the bodies, unaware of their discoveries. Corvainius was wanted for murder, and his sister was considered his accomplice. One night, he went out on a hunt alone, leaving his sister behind. While hiding in the forest, Corvainius failed to realize that the hunter was actually the hunted.

Corvainius waited quietly for an unsuspecting traveler to arrive when, suddenly, a large net weighted down by many anchors surrounded him, bringing him to his knees. Despite his increased strength, Corvainius was unable to remove the entire net but could take off one weight at a time. Before attempting to move, he found himself encircled by a group of twelve hunters. Corvainius felt both enraged and frightened by his predicament as he remembered his curse and the necessity of feeding to keep his sister alive.

"Well, well, well, look what we got here, boys. We bagged ourselves a murderer," said one hunter.

"Yeah, yeah, I've seen him around here before," said another.

Corvainius tried his hardest to fight his restraints but was unsuccessful. The hunters wrapped a chain around Corvainius and threw him into a cart nearby. He listened to the sounds of conversation about rewards for capturing him and how the king would be pleased to catch a murderer. Their conversations became dulled by the sounds of the creaking wheels as they headed towards the castle.

The cart came to an abrupt stop, and Corvainius knew they had not arrived at the castle yet. He overheard the hunters talk about keeping him in a barn for a couple of days before collecting the bounty reward. Corvainius was now terrified for his sister's safety, knowing that if he didn't feed by sunrise, his sister would die.

Lucky for Corvainius, the inside of the barn was dark and cold, and there were no signs of sunlight anywhere.

Time had seemed to drag on, and without being able to see any light in the barn, Corvainius was unable to tell how long he had been there. Corvainius saw his captors gathered at the far end of the barn and thought to himself, "*You should kill each other,*" and immediately, the sounds of swords being drawn rang out throughout the barn. The sound of swords clashing and men screaming filled the vacant space within the barn. Did Corvainius cause this to happen just by thinking about it? The pain in his stomach had become nearly unbearable, but Corvainius was determined to survive. "*You should release me,*" thought Corvainius, and within seconds, one of the hunters stood before him, soaked in blood, and began releasing his bonds.

As soon as he became free, Corvainius grabbed hold of the man and bit him with enough ferocity to tear out his throat. Fresh blood had never tasted so divine. What a relief he felt as the blood he drank coursed through his body. Immediately, Corvainius remembered his sister and, with caution, peered outside the doors of the barn and saw it was still dark.

Maybe it had only been a few hours or a few days. Corvainius wasn't sure of either one, but he knew for sure he had to hurry home to ensure his sister's safety.

Corvainius raced home as quickly as he could, moving with blinding speed out of fear for his sister's wellbeing. Upon arriving at his farm, a sinking feeling filled his chest. Searching through the darkness, he discovered what he believed to be a body lying in a field. Dreading the worst, Corvainius dashed over, only to make a heartbreaking discovery. It was indeed his sister lying in the field beside the house, and there were no traces of golden strands present.

His sister had lain face down before coming to a bitter and remorseless end. Her eyes were glazed over with an opaque white haze, and her lips were blue and cold. Dark veins on her body had begun to form from the coagulating blood. Her fingernails, which were once a vibrant pink color, were now a purplish black. Her mouth was agape, exposing a dark purple tongue and bluish gums.

Corvainius collapsed to his knees and released a tremendous scream of agony. Tears of blood began to fall from his eyes and pool in the dirt beneath him. He drove his fist into the dry earth repeatedly as a large plume of dirt engulfed him. Clutching his chest, Corvainius fell on his side in a fetal position and began to wail.

Despite all that he had done to protect his sister throughout his life, he now felt it was all in vain. Corvainius was ready to go to any lengths, even if it meant turning into a bloodthirsty creature of the night. He was overwhelmed not only by pain and deep remorse but also by a surge of uncontrollable rage. His sister had been the only thing keeping the monster within him at bay, and with her death, he felt that restraint had finally shattered.

Corvainius buried his sister beside the barn and then drenched his house in lamp oil before lighting it ablaze. He sat there and watched as every bit of memory he had there became engulfed in flame and would soon become ash. Crazed by fury and loneliness, Corvainius set out for a night of unrelenting slaughter. Running through the forest, he came upon a small cottage isolated in a clearing without any roads leading to it. He could hear voices from inside signaling a father, mother, and child. Corvainius had knocked upon the door, and when there was an answer, he requested to enter. After being granted permission to enter the dwelling, the killing began.

His blood lust and fury caused Coravinius to commit an uncontrollable slaughter. His first victim was the father, who had allowed him to enter the cottage. He had his throat ripped out by the swipe of Corvainius' hand, preventing his ability to scream as his blood was viciously consumed. Corvainius' next victim was the unsuspecting mother, for whom he tore out her throat savagely with his teeth and forced his hand into her rib cage, ripping her heart out.

His hunger was still unquenched, and his fury remained unsettled. His final victim was their young son, who had awakened to the sound of commotion as furniture was overturned. The boy rounded the corner to witness the bloodbath of his parents' slaughter and screamed. Being alerted of the boy's presence, Corvainius was left to commit the unforgivable atrocity of taking his life. While being ruthless, Corvainius sank his teeth deep into the flesh of the boy while listening to his screams. In order to silence the screams that had further enraged Corvainius, he shoved his hand into the boy's mouth and tore off his jaw, removing a part of his tongue with it.

The only clarity Corvainius had was to destroy the evidence of his massacre. So he lined the bodies in front of the fireplace before overloading them with a pile of broken furniture, causing the fire to spread around the room. Corvainius contemplated whether he should entrap himself inside the cottage to end his own life or if he felt that his killing spree wasn't yet finished.

Corvainius had become consumed by rage and hatred that he found impossible to control. The more his rage grew, the more his hunger for blood grew. The killings continued throughout the night, as merciless and savage as the one before. Each kill became easier and more detached as Corvainius relinquished his control to his rage.

When the sun began to rise, Corvainius realized he needed to find shelter quickly and discovered it in a nearby cave. Images of his deceased sister's body lying face down had seared themselves into his mind, driving him to the brink of madness. As time passed, his heart cracked off another small piece until he became completely heartless and feral. Before the sun had fully set, Corvainius heard the sound of a distant caravan approaching. Still bloodthirsty, he waited patiently, hoping they would stop for the night. Hearing the creaking wheels come to a halt, a smile began to creep across his lips.

The sun had finally set, and it was Corvainius's moment to hunt. He crept through the forest silently so as not to raise any alarms of his presence. He could hear the footsteps of an unsuspecting victim approaching and decided to take cover, hiding himself among the tall branches of a nearby tree. His vision was red from fury, and the glow of golden strands throughout the forest was scattered in all directions.

Unaware that he was being watched, a soldier wandered through the forest on patrol. When he came within mere feet of Corvainius, he was attacked by a surprise pounce that knocked him to the ground. Corvainius covered the soldier's mouth and sank his teeth deep into his neck. Thinking his attack was silent had raised suspicion among other soldiers in the area.

Before Corvainius could finish what he had started, he was forced to flee into the cover of darkness. As he escaped, he realized he was closing in on the caravan's location. Struggling to focus his vision, he saw something that made his fury dissipate entirely. A woman. Not just any random woman, but one who bore a strikingly uncanny resemblance to his sister, Cordelia.

He stood in the shadows and gazed at the woman, wondering if this was fate or a hallucination. As he watched her, he thought that this could be another chase to get his sister back in one form or another, and that made his heart begin to heal while his bloodlust faded into wonder. He had to have her and make her a vampire like him to keep the feeling of having his sister forever. "*This time, I will protect you,*" he thought to himself.

Chapter 8:
A New Life

As we neared the end of the forest, the road transitioned from gravel to cobblestone. The carriage began to sway to and fro as the wheels passed over the crevices between the stones. The road began to ascend a steep hill. Atop the hill, I could see small houses and shops. I could hear the ringing of a church bell in the air.

As we approached the summit, I could see how lively this quaint little town was. People were out and about, dashing from shop to shop with arms full of purchased goods. The carriage came to a stop in front of a large basilica that rose to heights that would make the trees of the forest pale in comparison.

Aedon opened the door to the carriage and guided me to my feet on the ground. Outside of the carriage, I was greeted by a petite, heavy woman.

"Hello, Your Royal Highness," greeted the woman. "I am Lady Agnes," she continued.

I held tightly to Aedon's hand as Lady Agnes escorted us inside. The cathedral's interior architecture was astonishing. Marble checkered tiles covered the floor, and carved wooden statues of angels adorned the main archway. Long stained glass windows lined the walls, while heavy timber beams stretched across the ceiling. Religious compositions were displayed against the back wall. Two large wooden doors stood on either side of the cathedral.

Aedon and Lady Agnes stepped away to discuss the order given by my father and to seek accommodations. After a while had passed, Lady Agnes and Aedon returned to escort me outside. I followed Lady Agnes while gripping Aedon's hand to a small cottage near the far east side of the village.

The cottage was white, with a moss-covered roof and wooden shingles. A rounded door stood between cross-hatched windows. Soft smoke curled from the chimney. After I opened the door, I followed Aedon inside. A long wooden table occupied the center of the room, with a chair at each end. A stone hearth rested against the side wall. A kettle hung from a hook on the mantle, overlooking a cast-iron cauldron. Bookshelves lined the back wall. At the other end of the cottage, a staircase led to an overhanging loft containing two beds draped in fur blankets. A small table with a candle sat between them. Tapestries hung from each side of the loft.

"This will be your new home for now," Aedon said.

"For how long? I want my father!" I demanded.

"I was ordered by your father to bring you here and keep you safe," answered Aedon.

"What am I supposed to do here?" I asked.

"You are to learn everything I teach you," answered Aedon.

"Some teacher you will be," I answered with sarcasm.

Aedon looked at me and began to smile.

"I see you have your father's stubbornness," he said.

I stormed up the stairs with a huff and sat on the bed with my arms crossed. Lady Agnes bid us goodnight before leaving us. Time passed, and the sun faded beyond the horizon, when a knock was heard at the door. I peered over the loft to see Aedon approach the door cautiously. When Aedon peeked through the door, I watched him pull it fully open, and a cloaked figure entered. Before I decided to move, the figure spoke in a voice that was all too familiar to me.

"Nathelia!" the figure called.

Before the figure could fully pull back the hood, I flew down the stairs and threw my arms around him.

"Papa!" I cried aloud.

"Oh my," Adeon murmured.

"Yes, my dear. I am here to see how you and Aedon are coming along," said my father.

Tears of joy flowed from my eyes as I held my father tight.

"I thought I was never going to see you again, Papa," I said as I wiped tears from my face.

"Sweetheart, I couldn't face walking this world without being able to see my special girl," my father said.

"How long am I to be here?" I asked.

"I am not sure right now, but I do know how to make a promise and keep it," stated my father.

"A promise? What promise?" I asked.

"I am going to make you a promise that I will come back here and see you every night until you can come back to the castle," said my father.

My father also surprised me with a bouquet of flowers. I sat them in the window behind the table. While holding my father's hand, I began escorting him around the cottage, showing him everything there was to see. My father stepped outside with Aedon to discuss matters I was too young to understand. I sat at the table and watched the fire flicker in the hearth.

Before long, the door opened, and both Aedon and my father came back inside. My father told me it was time for me to go to bed. After I lay down, he tucked me in and kissed my forehead. Shortly after he left, Aedon climbed into the other bed and snuffed out the candle.

It felt like I had only slept for a few minutes before being abruptly awakened by the sensation of drowning. As I quickly jumped out of bed, I saw Aedon holding a pail and laughing. I stood in shock, looking like a drowned rat as water pooled around my feet.

"Time for your chores," said Aedon with a chuckle. "You will go to the stables to brush and wash Despair," he continued. "Ugh!" I screamed in anger as I stomped down the stairs to change clothes. After I changed, I made my way to the stables near the front of the village. Despair was joyful to see me. I fed him a small handful of oats before I began to brush him. His coat shone with every stroke. Dust started to fill the air from long, vigorous journeys.

I felt the feeling of someone watching me. I looked across the stables to catch a glimpse of a boy's head peering over the back of a chestnut thoroughbred. Within a split second, he disappeared behind the horse, and I looked under Despair to see two legs under the mare. I felt annoyed and walked over with a wet sponge in my hand. When I walked around the mare, I saw the boy trying to hide behind it, so I threw the wet sponge at him.

"Do you mind telling me as to why you are being so rude by staring?" I asked.

"My apologies, I didn't mean to stare," he replied with a sense of uneasiness.

"What is your name?" I said with a hint of authority.

"My name is Artheus. What is your name?" he asked.

"Nathelia. I am the daughter of-" I began to reply.

"Who is your friend?" asked Aedon, coming around the stables.

"He is not my friend! He is a rude boy who likes to stare!" I declared, stomping my foot on the ground.

"Oh, is that so?" asked Aedon with a smile of amusement.

"HE IS NOT MY FRIEND!" I screamed and stomped back to Despair.

Aedon followed behind and leaned towards me.

"You like that boy, don't you?" Aedon whispered.

"No way! Ugh!" I yelled.

I could feel myself blushing as heat began to grow around my cheeks. I splashed water at Aedon and stomped back to the cottage in embarrassment. Aedon walked behind me, and I could feel his smiling face peering over my shoulder.

I entered the cottage and slammed the door behind me.

Seconds later, Aedon entered with a smile still on his face.

"He likes you, you know?" Aedon said.

"You don't know what you're talking about!" I declared.

"I was watching, and I can tell he fancies you," he said.

I ran upstairs, buried my face in the bed, and screamed. Aedon remained downstairs to unpack a satchel on the table. While Aedon was out, he had purchased rabbit meat and vegetables for a stew. I was so embarrassed, not because of what Aedon said, but because it was true.

After some time had passed, Aedon called me downstairs to eat. When I walked down the stairs, I saw him scooping food into two wooden bowls. Aedon looked up at me and began to fight back a smile, but I noticed.

"What?" I asked.

"Nothing," he said.

"You're lying," I stated.

"I know you like that boy and-" he began.

"You don't know anything!" I protested.

"Don't worry, your secret is safe with me," Aedon said, running his thumb and index finger across his lips.

The sun had gone down, and there was a knock on the door.

It opened. My father stood in the doorway.

"Is there enough for one more?" my father asked.

"There is always enough for your majesty," Aedon said, bowing to my father.

Aedon prepared another bowl of stew for my father, who had pulled up another chair beside me and sat down.

"So, is everything going well here?" my father inquired.

"Yes, your majesty," Aedon answered. "Nathelia learned how to bathe and groom Despair," he continued.

When Aedon said this, my heart began to race, and my palms began to sweat. The anxiety was swelling inside me.

"Is that so?" my father turned to me and asked.

"Why yes, Papa. Aedon is an excellent teacher," I said with a nervous smile.

"That's wonderful. You know he was my teacher when I was your age," said my father.

"No, I didn't," I answered.

"Speaking of learning… I am tired. Adeon has taught me a lot today, and I am ready for bed," I continued.

"Okay, my dear, run along, and I will be behind you to tuck you in," my father said.

I rushed up the stairs, dove into bed, and listened to the sound of my father's boots climbing the stairs. My father approached the bed, pulled the blanket up to my chin, and sat on the edge of the bed. With a tight hug and a kiss on my forehead, my father wished me goodnight. As he reached the top of the stairs, I sat up and called for him.

"I love you, papa," I declared.

"I love you too, my dearest Nathelia," he replied.

After a brief exchange with Aedon, my father left. Shortly after, Aedon climbed the stairs, and I insisted that he tell me what he had said to my father.

"I did not disclose your secret if that's what you want to know," he answered.

"Good," I stated matter-of-factly, which made Aedon smile.

"What seems to be so funny?" I asked.

"Nothing, Your Royal Highness. Goodnight," Aedon replied.

I lay awake, staring at the ceiling while thinking about Artheus. He was only a couple of years older than me. His hair was blonde, and his skin was sun-kissed from hours of doing chores under the hot sun. His eyes were icy blue, conveying a look of comfort and security. He was tall for his age, and he looked strong. What felt like moments of sleep had actually been hours, as I was startled awake by Aedon. I looked outside the window and saw that the sun had begun to rise.

"I need you to go and feed hay to Despair," Aedon instructed.

Without a word, I changed clothes and headed to the stables. I was nervous that Artheus would see me, but the coast was clear. I grabbed a handful of hay and began to feed it to Despair when I heard a voice that made me want to dive into the water trough.

"Hey, Nathelia," said Artheus behind me. I slowly turned to face him and began to feel myself blush.

'H-h-hi- "I stuttered.

"So…so what's your horse's name?" asked Artheus nervously. I turned back toward Despair and continued feeding him hay.

"His name is Despair, and he isn't my horse," I said with a hint of attitude.

"I wanted to ask you a question, but I am afraid you might throw a sponge at me," said Artheus cautiously.

"Be swift with your words, or I might," I said, unable to face him due to the smile on my face.

"I was wondering if you wanted to go on a ride with me around the village," asked Artheus.

I turned around to answer him and noticed Aedon hiding behind a wall and nodding in approval.

"I think I can do that, but first," I answered as I reached for a sponge and hurled it at Artheus.

"I thought you said-," Artheus began to say.

"I said I might throw a sponge at you, and I decided to do so," I said with a bashful smile.

Artheus smiled and started to blush.

"Meet me here after I finish my chores, and we will ride together," I stated.

"As you wish," said Artheus before dashing up the road.

I quickly finished my chores, ran back to the cottage, and changed into a clean dress. When I returned to the stables, I noticed that Despair had already been saddled and armored with a rolled parchment tied to the breastplate. I unrolled the note, and I read it. It stated…

Please ride Despair on your journey. I will stay close enough to keep you safe, and Despair will protect you. Signed S.A.

Sir Aedon. I knew it! I looked around and couldn't see Aedon, but I knew he was somewhere nearby. Shortly after, I noticed Artheus approaching the stables. I watched him as he saddled the chestnut mare. After he had finished, he mounted the horse and adjusted himself to the saddle.

"Are you ready to go?" Artheus asked.

"Uh, yes. Give me a sec," I said.

I attempted to climb onto Despair and fell onto my back. A soft snicker came from a pile of hay in the corner. It had to be Aedon.

"Here, let me help," Artheus began.

I heard a quiet whistle, and Despair lowered himself to the ground. Artheus offered a hand and helped me climb into the saddle. I then heard two quiet clicks, and Despair stood to his feet.

"What was that noise?" asked Artheus.

"I didn't hear anything," I lied.

Artheus shrugged his shoulders and climbed upon his horse once more.

"So, what is your horse's name?" I asked.

"Her name is Dreamer," answered Artheus.

"She's beautiful," I declared.

As Artheus and Dreamer rode by, Despair began to follow. I rode alongside Artheus around the edge of the village, feeling the warm sun on my skin and a gentle breeze against me as Despair lifted me up. Artheus halted his horse beneath a tree and dismounted. He tied the reins to a low-hanging branch.

I attempted to dismount Despair, but my dress became caught in the stirrups, and I lost my balance. Before I fell to the ground, Artheus caught me, and we tumbled together. Looking at each other and realizing the situation we put each other in, we began to laugh. He helped me to my feet and tied Despair to the same branch as Dreamer.

As Despair and Dreamer grazed beneath the trees, Artheus took my hand and walked me under the branches, where we lay on our backs and watched the leaves billow in the breeze. We began pointing out shapes in the clouds that resembled animals. Artheus sat up and carved our initials into the side of the tree with a small dagger, telling me it made our friendship eternal.

After spending most of the day with him, he helped me to my feet and walked me back to Despair. I knew I couldn't mount him in my dress, so I tried to whistle like I had heard Aedon do. Even though it was poorly executed, Despair still lowered himself to the ground and let me climb into the saddle.

I clicked my tongue twice, and Despair stood. I was so impressed that it had worked. I sat with the posture of pure arrogance. Artheus had untied Despair and Dreamer before mounting his own saddle. He began to head back, and I looked towards the trees, noticing Aedon standing beside a tree, smiling.

I gave a wave of appreciation and continued on the ride back to the stables. When we arrived back at the stables, Artheus began to unsaddle Dreamer as I whistled for Despair to lower himself. I dismounted and clicked for him to stand. I watched Artheus remove the saddle from Dreamer and hang it on the wall behind him.

After Dreamer was fully stripped down, Artheus promised to meet me again the next day and ran home. I began to loosen the saddle from Despair when Aedon approached from the shadows across the street.

"I take it that you enjoyed yourself?" Aedon announced. I was so frightened by him that I screamed.

"DON'T DO THAT!" I screamed.

"Do what?" said Aedon, laughing at my terror.

"Sneak up on me," I said while trying to catch my breath.

"I didn't mean to put you in such fear, Your Royal Highness," apologized Aedon.

"Well, you did! I thought I was going to die," I chuckled back.

We both stood and laughed at one another. Aedon assisted me with removing Despair's saddle and armor.

"Have you told him yet?' Aedon asked. I thought for a moment before I realized what he meant.

"No. And you're not going to either," I snapped.

"Of course, Your Royal Highness. I wouldn't think of it," replied Aedon. "But I think you should tell him."

"Maybe I will, maybe I won't," I stated smugly.

"As you wish. By the way, I noticed that you are good with Despair," said Aedon.

"I knew that was you in the hay," I said, nudging Aedon's arm. Aedon said nothing. He just looked at me and smiled.

"Thank you for helping me get onto Despair earlier," I said.

"I don't know what you speak of," said Aedon as his smile became a grin. Aedon chuckled as we both headed back towards the cottage.

Chapter 9:
Light Shines Through Death's Veil

Artheus was cast into a world of tragedy. When he was born, his mother died from complications, leaving his father alone to raise him. Burdened by devastating pain in his heart, Artheus' father blamed him for his mother's death. Unable to confront the pain and unwilling to raise him as a father should, Artheus was cast aside and abandoned on the steps of a church in a town called Glovendall.

Artheus had never had the chance to meet and know his father. A family adopted him with the help of the town abbess, Lady Agnes. Artheus was placed into a warm, loving home with a couple who had found themselves struggling to conceive a child. The couple who had taken him in were named Josaline and Erion. According to the locals in the town, it was unknown who Artheus' parents were.

Josaline made a living as a seamstress and opened a shop with her husband in town. They crafted dresses, shirts, and many other pieces of clothing. Despite their lack of status, they often wore the finest fabrics, which almost led others to perceive them as royalty.

While growing up in Glovendall, Artheus developed a fascination for horses. On his eighth birthday, Artheus was given a gift that surpassed his very own imagination: a horse. Not just any horse but a beautiful chestnut mare. Artheus found himself bewitched by its majestic beauty. He never imagined that a creature like this could possibly have existed.

Never before had Artheus seen such a magnificent creature. Heavy, dense muscle draped her long legs, and her fur shone in the sunlight as if she had been chiseled from solid amber. Her thick red mane reminded him of hot coals raked over a fire. She had hazel eyes and carried a warm glow reflecting the sunlight.

Artheus pressed his ear to her chest and listened to the rhythmic beating of her heart. Her fur was warm in the sunlight, and she smelled of fresh wood chips and grass. Even though she towered over young Artheus, he was not afraid. He was more excited than he had ever been.

Eager to ride, he led her to a low-hanging rail in the stables and started climbing it to mount the horse. The couple who raised him, whom he saw as his parents, observed as Artheus finally settled atop the mare. He felt elated, unable to conceal his joy while perched high on the horse's back.

"Do you like her?" asked his parents.

"It's like a dream. I love her," he answered.

"I believe Dreamer would be a fitting name for her then," suggested his parents.

He set out to an open field where he put Dreamer through her paces. As she raced across the open field, Artheus' chest began to tingle with excitement. He came to a stop under a tree and tied the reins to a low-hanging branch. While Dreamer grazed upon the tall grass, Artheus lay on his back and gazed upwards towards the skies. He watched as the clouds passed by in the shapes of animals and buildings. He began telling Dreamer wild fantasies about monsters and princesses. Artheus sat up, propping himself on his elbows, and noticed a man standing in the woodline watching him.

The man seemed familiar from somewhere deep in his mind. He casually shook off the notion and decided to head back into town, where his parents would be waiting for him. After reuniting with his parents, Artheus never mentioned the man he had seen earlier. The question continued to linger in his mind: *"Why did that man seem so familiar?"* Artheus resolved to ignore any ideas he might have had about the man and carried on with his daily life, telling himself it was just a fleeting moment and not to let it consume him.

Each day, Artheus had to groom and care for Dreamer by feeding and bathing her. He didn't mind this because it gave him the opportunity to admire the horse he had fallen in love with. He had dreamed of having his own horse for years, after spending countless hours watching people around town come and go on horseback. It all seemed like a dream come true. Every day after finishing his chores, Artheus would ride Dreamer to the same tree he had sat beneath before, hoping to see the mysterious man again. Days passed by, and still, there was no sight of the mysterious man, which made Artheus begin to question his sanity.

After a few weeks had passed, the mysterious man appeared, but this time, instead of being in the woodline, he was in the middle of the village with a young girl. Artheus confirmed to himself that he hadn't imagined seeing the man, and it piqued his curiosity. The girl, however, changed him in ways he would have never thought of.

The girl was an auburn-haired beauty who, at first glance, took Artheus's breath away. His chest started to tingle with excitement, and his palms began to sweat. He found himself mesmerized by the sheer extravagance she possessed. Seeing someone so beautiful told him that she was not from around here. His heart raced in his chest.

In his mind, Artheus knew that he had to know more about this girl. Artheus just watched from a distance as the man and the girl made their way through the village towards the stables. Who was she? He had to know.

Arthus made the decision to remain distant and not be seen. He decided to conceal himself amongst the pile of hay inside the stables and awaited the arrival of the man and the girl. Peering through the hay, he watched the girl walk past with mesmerizing elegance. He noticed that Lady Agnes accompanied both the man and the girl. Artheus watched from the stables as they approached a nearby cottage.

Artheus waited in the stables to see if the man and the girl, along with Lady Agnes, would re-emerge from the cottage. Time passed, and when the door opened, only Lady Agnes appeared. His curiosity started to get the better of him, so he decided to approach Lady Agnes to ask who the man and the girl were.

"Lady Agnes, can I ask you a question?" asked Artheus.

"Of course, my child," replied Lady Agnes.

"Who was the man and girl that I saw walking by a moment ago?" asked Artheus.

"The man you had seen was a knight named Aedon, and the girl you had seen was the King's daughter," answered Lady Agnes.

Artheus decided to hurry home and reflect on the new information that Lady Agnes had shared with him. The fact that the King's daughter would be in that town came as a complete shock to Artheus. Regardless of who the girl was, he realized that he had developed feelings he had yet to understand. He found himself entranced by the sheer magnificence of her beauty. Never had he imagined encountering an actual princess.

The following day, things seemed normal, and Artheus began completing his chores. As fantasies swam through the back of his mind, Artheus was completely unprepared for what was yet to come. He noticed a second horse that he didn't recognize in the stables beside Dreamer. It was nearly mid-morning, and an unsuspected opportunity arose before him.

From the opposite of Dreamer, Artheus spotted the amber-haired beauty approaching from the other side of the stables. He was determined to make contact with her, but he was unsure about addressing a princess. He pretended to continue grooming Dreamer as he admired her from across the stables. He had hoped that his admiration wasn't noticeable, but before he could even speak, it was too late.

"Do you mind telling me as to why you are being so rude by staring?" she asked.

"My apologies, I didn't mean to stare," he replied with a sense of uneasiness.

"What is your name?" she said with a hint of authority.

"My name is Artheus. What is your name?" he asked.

"Nathelia, and I am the daughter of-" she began to reply.

"Who is your friend?" asked the knight Artheus had seen the day before accompanying Natheilia.

"He is not my friend! He is a rude boy who likes to stare!" she declared, stomping her foot on the ground.

To Artheus, her behavior was more curious than anything else, which attracted him to her even more. Even when she pouted in embarrassment, he still found her remarkably beautiful. He was determined to be her friend and dreamed of one day marrying her. Artheus reminded himself that these were just foolish fantasies and that a girl like her, a princess, would never find herself interested in a boy like him.

Artheus eventually built a rapport with her, and they soon became friends. He found that they both shared a similar interest in horses. Every day, they would ride out into the open field and lie underneath a tree at its center. Both of them would lie on their backs in the tall grass and gaze at the sky. They would point to different clouds and tell one another what they believed they looked like. As time went on, Artheus and Natheilia would find themselves giggling and laughing at one another over the most immature reasons.

Artheus couldn't have dreamed of a happier life than one with her. It seemed as if the years had flown by since the first day they had met. The more time they spent together, the more comfortable Artheus and Natheilia became from being in each other's presence. Artheus felt as though his dreams of loving her for eternity were foolish and inconceivable. But for the moments that he had, it was definitely a dream come true. As Artheus grew more comfortable, his boldness also grew, until one day he decided to give her a kiss on the cheek.

He was afraid of how Natheilia would respond to it, but Artheus felt as though he had nothing to lose. Instead of reacting in absolute disgust, Natheilia accepted it willingly with a slight blush. In his mind, he only hoped that his feelings towards her would become reciprocated. He knew what his feelings for her were but found himself too afraid to tell her. With every waking day, his love for her grew even stronger.

After some time, Artheus was roused by alarming news. There was a knock at his door, and upon opening it, he found Aedon waiting. Aedon shared the troubling news of the king's disappearance and requested a private conversation with Artheus. A sudden wave of fear engulfed Artheus, accompanied by a nauseating sensation in his stomach.

Gathering his courage to speak with Aedon, he stepped outside into the night. Artheus was afraid of Aedon due to his towering size and appearance. Even though he had been around him for years, neither of them had decided to speak to one another until that night. The news that Aedon had relayed to Artheus left him in shock and disbelief. It also caused his heart to break.

"I have to tell you something that I have waited a long time for," said Aedon.

"Please don't hurt me," pleaded Artheus in fear.

"What? No!" Aedon responded, confused.

"I thought you were going to hurt me because I'm in love with Natheilia," Artheus replied cautiously.

"No, I would never. I needed to tell you about who you are," said Aedon with a slight smirk on his face.

"Who am I? What do you mean?" Artheus inquired.

"I am your brother," answered Aedon.

The news hit Artheus like an oncoming mountain. He was in disbelief and couldn't comprehend what he had been told. Brother? After all this time, Aedon waited to tell him now. There had to be some sort of mistake.

"My brother? How can this be?" Artheus demanded.

"Our mother died while giving birth to you," replied Aedon.

"Is that why I was adopted?" Artheus asked.

"No, you were adopted because our father couldn't handle the loss of our mother and blamed you for it," answered Aedon with his head hung low.

"Who was she, and will I ever meet our father?" Artheus asked in curiosity.

Aedon conveyed the heartbreaking news of their father's death, revealing that raiders had killed him years earlier. He explained to Artheus how he discovered their father had been an assassin for the king, a revelation that inspired Aedon to follow the same path. He also shared his love for his late wife, Devina, who was the queen's aunt. Aedon recounted her tragic death and revealed she had been pregnant with their daughter at the time, a baby who did not survive.

Artheus was heartbroken by the news about his family and apologized to Aedon for having to endure such heartache. Artheus never regretted the family that raised him, and discovering his biological parents only made him appreciate them even more. The people he considered parents were the best he could have ever dreamed of having. Still, being abandoned due to his father's heartache and inability to resolve his emotional conflict weighed heavily on Artheus's heart. Despite that, Artheus found it a relief to finally know the truth and learn that he had a brother.

Aedon informed Artheus that his parents were instructed to take him to the castle to train him to become an assassin like him. The idea of going to the castle was very enticing to him, but the thought of leaving Natheilia behind hurt him even more than learning about his parents. The continuous emotional blows of heartache began to pound at Artheus. This was a challenge that he didn't feel prepared to face. On one hand, the prospect of being an assassin seemed exhilarating. But on the other hand, leaving behind his love felt unbearable.

"Can I at least say goodbye?" asked Artheus.

"There isn't any time. You and your family must leave for the castle at once," Aedon instructed.

"Why is it so pertinent that I leave now?" asked Artheus.

"The king is missing, and if I have to join in a search for him, I want to appoint you to take charge of Natheilias' safety," Aedon explained.

"Take charge?" inquired Artheus.

"If something were to ever happen to me, it would be up to you to look after and care for Natheilia," Aedon answered.

"So why me?" questioned Artheus.

"With how much I know that you love her, you are the only one I trust to keep her safe for the sake of the crown," Aedon clarified.

This responsibility became a heavy task for Artheus. Regardless, he was willing to take it. As much as he loved Natheilia, Artheus was willing to move mountains for her.

As much as it pained him to do so, Artheus wanted to do what was best for Natheilia. *'I love you, and I will return for you,'* Artheus thought to himself.

Artheus ran inside his house and helped his parents pack all their belongings. Aedon stayed outside and watched as they did. After all their possessions were fully packed and loaded upon a cart, Artheus and his parents began their journey towards the castle. As they passed the cottage that Natheilia lived in, Artheus blew a kiss and promised himself that he would come back for her. Inside the cottage, the flickering light of a candle emanated through the window.

Artheus continued to gaze at the cottage until it vanished from sight, wishing that Natheilia would step outside and permit him to bid farewell with a kiss. As the cottage appeared to shrink with distance, Artheus's heart continued to break. Memories and images of Natheilia swirled through his mind as he and his family continued their journey. Artheus realized that all he had to remind him of Natheilia were fleeting memories, but nevertheless, these were memories he would treasure for the rest of his life.

Hours passed, but it seemed like mere minutes to Artheus, who fantasized about Natheilia. With a jarring thud of the cart, Artheus was snapped back to reality. They had arrived at the castle. At the entrance, Artheus' father produced a folded piece of parchment that he had not seen before. A soldier approached them and accepted the piece of parchment from Artheus' father. Upon reading its contents, another soldier was ordered to open the gate and allow passage. Another soldier escorted them into the castle grounds.

Artheus was curious about what the parchment contained, but didn't entertain the idea of asking. They were escorted to an inner cottage situated within the castle walls. It was quaint, but it reminded Artheus of the cottage in which Natheilia lived. This made Artheus feel closer to her, even though he knew he would be away for a long time. Artheus and his parents unloaded their belongings inside, and the soldier told Artheus to follow him.

Artheus parted ways with his parents after a long, warm embrace and began to cross the courtyard. Small shops lined the outer edges of the courtyard, but no vendors were present. Several small fires burned on the ground, and women and children who lived either inside the castle walls or nearby huddled around them. The faces of the individuals that Artheus saw showed signs of poverty and famine.

A woman wrapped in cloaks tried to breastfeed her crying child. Many people he passed met Artheus's gaze as he made his way across the courtyard. Their stares made him shudder. Before long, Artheus and the soldier arrived at a wooden door at the side of the courtyard. With a single knock from the soldier, the door opened into a pitch-black hallway.

Artheus stepped inside and found himself being escorted by yet another soldier. As his eyes adjusted to the darkness, Artheus could see that he was walking down a long stone hallway with low ceilings. The sound of their footsteps echoed down the hall as they arrived at a small room where he was to be fitted with armor. A man measured his body with strands of cloth and laid the cut pieces on a nearby table. Artheus was later escorted back to the cottage with his parents for the night.

When the sun rose the following morning, Artheus and his family were awakened by a loud knock on the door. Upon opening the door, Artheus saw two soldiers who stood ready to escort him to another part of the castle. After getting dressed, Artheus followed the soldiers across the courtyard and through another door. This time, the hallway was slightly larger, and the ceilings weren't so low.

Burning torches hung from the walls and were spaced evenly along the hallway.

Despite the several blazing torches, Artheus still sensed the lingering chill of the stones as he navigated through the hallway. It appeared almost infinite, featuring numerous twists and turns along the way. Eventually, Artheus arrived at the end of the serpentine corridor where a huge wooden door with iron fittings stood. Upon opening the door, Artheus glimpsed a vast corridor beyond.

Inside the corridor, men were scattered throughout the room, training with either weapons or in hand-to-hand combat. The sound of clashing metal rang throughout the room. Men wrestled one another and swung what looked like heavy weapons. The air stank of men and sweat. An older yet large gentleman approached Artheus to greet him.

"I'm Garvon. I will be your instructor," the man greeted.

"Hello, I'm-" Artheus began.

"I know who you are. I trained your brother Aedon," interrupted Garvon.

"You know my brother?" asked Artheus.

"Yes, yes. I trained him into the fearless assassin he is today," Garvon answered.

"I hope I can be as good an assassin as he is," declared Artheus.

"Of course, my boy, with some training and nourishment in your belly, we will make you into a great assassin just like him," Garvon said while making playful jabs at Artheus' stomach.

Artheus was amazed at the skill the other men displayed and seemed slightly overwhelmed, but decided to remain focused. Artheus was led across the room to another boy who was slightly older than him. He could see that the boy was toned. Sweat droplets were scattered upon him, and his hair glistened in the light from the torches. His hands were scarred and bruised from years of intense training.

His face was smeared with dirt, and his expression was intent during his training. His eyes seemed as if his gaze could pierce through solid iron. Artheus started to feel slightly intimidated by the boy and envious of his physique. Artheus was thoroughly impressed by the skill of all the men in the room and how they appeared tireless during their intense training regimens.

"This will be your training partner, Xandor," Garvon announced.

"Are you ready, kid?" asked Xandor.

"Yes, my brother Aedon-" Artheus began.

"I know Aedon. I'm his nephew," interjected Xandor.

"Wait! Nephew?" Artheus Asked.

"You had a half-brother from your mom before she met your father," explained Xandor.

"Did you know my father?" Artheus asked curiously.

"I never met him, but I heard of him. He was an assassin for the king years ago," answered Xandor.

"So, is your father here at the castle?" Artheus inquired.

"Sadly, no. He passed away two years ago after being poisoned," clarified Xandor.

"I'm so sorry," Artheus apologized.

"Don't sweat it. He was a cruel man anyway," said Xandor.

Artheus was truly amazed. He never imagined meeting his own nephew and training with him. Nor did he envision having a half-brother. Knowing that he had actual family at the castle made things feel less empty for Artheus. He planned to train hard and learn as quickly as possible in order to return to Natheilia.

"Have you ever been in a fight before?" asked Xandor.

"Well, no, but I did have the princess throw a sponge at me once," Artheus answered.

Both Xandor and Artheus started to laugh hysterically at each other. Artheus began to realize just how safe his life had been, as he had never been in a fight before. As ridiculous as it seemed, Artheus was almost glad he had never had to fight. However, things for him were soon going to change.

"So you're telling me that you haven't even been punched before?" asked Xandor.

"Nope," Artheus said, smiling.

Without warning, Xandor swung his arm and drove his fist as hard as he could into Artheus's face. Artheus barely saw it coming, and by the time he did, it was too late to react. He felt Xandor's fist dig deep into his flesh, and his vision began to blur. A throbbing pain started to grow where Xandor had punched him. Artheus's eyes watered, and when he looked down, drops of blood were falling to the floor.

"Ouch! That hurt," Artheus cried.

"It wasn't meant to feel good. But now you have had your first punch and know what to expect," answered Xandor.

"You could have given me some notice before doing that," Artheus barked.

"You won't always have the luxury of receiving a warning when you're in combat," Xandor explained.

"I oughta punch you back," said Artheus.

"Go ahead and take your best shot," taunted Xandor.

Artheus reared back his fist and threw a devastating punch to the side of Xandor's face, which ultimately bounced off like a wet potato. Xandor didn't even flinch, and Artheus' hand throbbed painfully. This was the first time Artheus had ever punched anything in his life. He hadn't imagined it would hurt him more than it hurt the one receiving the blow. Artheus found himself clutching his hand and wincing in pain.

"Are you ok?" asked Xandor.

"My hand hurts," Artheus replied.

"Did you hit me as hard as you could?" Xandor asked.

"Of course," Artheus answered ashamedly.

"Well, we are definitely going to work on that," stated Xandor.

After receiving his first punch, Artheus no longer felt out of place. He learned that the reason his own punch was not as effective was due to poor execution and incorrect technique. Artheus and Xandor trained countless hours each day, refining their combat skills. At the end of each day, Artheus would return to the cottage sore and bruised, having endured significant pain throughout his training.

A couple of years after Artheus began his training, odd occurrences started to unfold. On a cool morning, the alarm bells within the castle chimed, waking Artheus from his sleep. He quickly got dressed and rushed out the door to find the source of the alarm. A huddled crowd of people stood in the courtyard, surrounding something or someone.

Soldiers began to force their way into the center of the group, and Artheus followed.

When Artheus reached the center, he saw the deceased body of an old man lying in a puddle of blood. At first, Artheus didn't recognize the man, but after further inspection, he immediately knew who it was. It was Garvon. It seemed as though his throat had been viciously ripped from his body. In his hand, he was still clutching a dagger. His eyes were foggy, and a look of pain was etched on his face.

Artheus had never seen a dead body before. He was horrified. There wasn't enough training in the world that could have prepared him for this precise moment. He stood frozen as soldiers cleared the crowd and inspected the body. Artheus saw Xandor standing across from him, wearing an expression of horror that mirrored his own.

Garvon's body was picked up and carried by soldiers to an unknown portion of the castle. A meeting was called; all trainees were to assemble in the training room. Artheus and Xandor made their way to the room and didn't speak a word about what they had just witnessed. When they entered the training room, Artheus could see the other trainees lined up, waiting for the arrival of the next appointed master assassin.

Hours passed before the door to the training room opened, allowing the new master assassin to enter. Artheus realized it was none other than Aedon. He desperately wanted to rush across the room and start asking questions about Natheilia, but fought hard to suppress the urge. Aedon announced his new role as the master assassin and said that someone else would take his place during his absence.

After the announcement, Artheus found it impossible not to ask Aedon about Natheilia. Aedon reassured him that she was in good health and had spoken about him every day. With Artheus' mind finally at ease, he found it more than rewarding to focus on his training. He and Xandor had grown more and more proficient with the use of weapons and hand-to-hand combat.

Over the years, Artheus had developed considerable muscle density. His height had increased and surpassed Xandor's. Xandor and Artheus were not just family; they had also become best friends. They trained together and ate together. They created games during training to maintain the excitement. They would bet against each other on who could perform better at specific tasks.

Years had passed, and Aedon had stopped visiting as regularly as he had before. Artheus would only see him occasionally. Each time they met, Aedon would update Artheus with any recent news concerning Natheilia and would ask if there was anything he wanted Aedon to convey to her. The day before Xandor and Artheus were set to graduate from their training, Artheus received devastating news.

A soldier handed him a handwritten letter from Natheilia, informing him that his brother Aedon had passed away and that his funeral would be within the week. Artheus's eyes began to fill with tears as he read the letter. He could smell her scent on the parchment, which he found comforting. He knew immediately what it was and what he was instructed to do if anything ever happened to Aedon.

'I'm coming. My love for it has been far too long.'

Chapter 10:
From Frozen Winters to Hell Gate

My father would often join us for dinner at my house, and each time he came, he would bring along flowers or some other small gift for me. One winter night, however, he completely surprised me with a puppy. I was in disbelief; I had never imagined receiving anything so adorable. As he walked in, I heard the soft whimpering sound that hinted at his surprise.

He carried a satchel over his shoulder, and when he opened it, I was even more amazed. Instead of just one puppy, there were two! One was a male, and the other was a female, both of whom were Great Danes.

"What will you name them?" my father asked.

"I will name this one, Bane," I said, holding the male.

Aedon picked up the female, and she peered at his chest. Both my father and I began to howl in laughter. Aedon did not seem to have the same amusement.

"I think Tyranny would be the perfect name for this one," Aedon said.

Again, Father and I began to howl. But to be honest, I agreed, and the names became permanent. Bane and Tyranny. The cutest puppies I could have ever envisioned. The puppies were both as black as a thick forest at midnight.

Their fur shone in the light like an onyx gem. I could see that their eyes were a frosty blue, similar to that of my mother's. With every whimper, I noticed their pink tongues hiding behind snowy white teeth. Tyranny had a black heart-shaped mark on her pink stomach.

Both Bane and Tyranny had little round bellies. I could see the off-white crust of dried milk from a recent feeding. I noticed that they had large paws with soft pink pads. I could smell the scent of their breath, tinged with milk. I lay on the floor and let Bane and Tyranny waddle toward me and begin to lick my face, which sent me into fits of laughter due to their little yet long tongues.

"These are now your responsibility," my father stated.

"Yes, Papa," I replied while laughing.

"If you raise them properly, they will grow to protect you," added my father. "Anything that you need will be provided, but care will come from you."

I leaped to my feet and threw my arms around my father. With a kiss on his cheek, I thanked him.

"I believe it is time for you to go to bed," said my father.

I carried Bane and Tyranny under each arm as I made my way up the stairs. As I lay in the bed, both Bane and Tyranny curled up at my feet. I began to fade into a dream when I heard one of the puppies whimpering. I sat up and didn't see Bane or Tyranny on the bed. I sprang from bed in search of them and could hear one of them growling. After looking under the bed, I spotted Tyranny dragging one of Aedon's large boots underneath the bed.

I pulled Tyranny from under the bed, where she was clinging tightly to Aedon's boot and growling. I placed the boot back in front of the bed and noticed Bane's plump belly and back legs sticking out of the other boot. His little legs kicked wildly, and his whines turned into howls. After placing Tyranny on the bed, I moved on to rescue Bane from the boot of doom.

Throughout all of this, Aedon did not stir. After I got the puppies back on the bed, I drifted off to sleep. When I woke up the next morning, I saw that both Bane and Tyranny were gone. I also noticed that Aedon was missing as well. I leaned over the edge of the bed and looked underneath... nothing.

I rushed to get dressed and fled down the stairs to find Aedon sitting on the floor, playing with Bane and Tyranny. Aedon had a boyish look of glee on his face. This was the first time I had ever witnessed real humanity from him. Aedon just seemed so gentle and blissful as the puppies ran around and climbed all over him.

My face broke into a smile I knew I couldn't hide. I just stood there and watched as Aedon sat on the floor, playfully growling at the puppies and playing tug-of-war with a glove. For a mammoth of a man who instilled fear in most with his mere appearance, I was witnessing a truly gentle side I had never known existed.

It was also the first time I had ever seen Aedon's hands. They were covered in scars from numerous battles. I could only imagine the stories each of them could tell. I never really felt as warm about Aedon as I did today. I admit that I have played jokes on him as he has played on me.

This was a different side of him that I never imagined. Even though he was intimidating and a trained assassin for my father, he was happy and laughing. If I had never known Aedon for who he really was, at this moment, I would have thought of him as a pure, kind, and gentle man. I cleared my throat to announce my presence. Quickly, Aedon jumped to his feet and cleared his throat, pretending that I didn't just see him displaying a softness for Bane and Tyranny. As he brushed himself off and put his glove back on, I watched Aedon's expression return to the same cold glare I had always known.

"Time for you to tend to Despair," Aedon announced.

"Of course," I replied.

I walked out the door to tend to my morning chores and noticed both Bane and Tyranny hopping behind me in an attempt to keep up. I found it amusing to watch as their ears flopped with every stride. When I reached the stables, I noticed that Artheus was already there and was busy brushing Dreamer. He seemed so content, and he hadn't noticed I was there. His attention was broken when Bane and Tyranny began to pull at his boots. I let out a muffled chuckle, which made Artheus finally notice that I was there.

"Oh, hi Nathelia, are these pups yours?" asked Artheus.

"Yes, they are mine," I giggled.

"They seem quite effective with their razor-sharp teeth." He smiled. "Please, let me go!" Artheus pleaded while trying to shake the jaw-locked Bane clinging to his boot.

"I am so sorry for their obscene wickedness," I apologized while trying to pull the puppies away from Artheus.

"If they keep up this ferociousness, I believe they could grow up to fight a bear," stated Artheus.

"Maybe," I said with a laugh.

After grooming and bathing both Dreamer and Despair, I found Aedon to ask him if I could ride Despair, and he gave me permission. Artheus helped me put the saddle and other tack onto Despair. Before we left, Aedon came by to collect Bane and Tyranny. When Aedon picked each of them up, I saw both Bane and Tyranny writhing and trying to chew aggressively at Aedon's gloves.

Artheus and I rode out to the same tree as we did almost every day and lay beneath its leaves. We talked and laughed for what felt like forever. Unexpectedly, Artheus turned to me and gave me a kiss on the cheek. I could feel my cheeks warm up, and a smile started to spread. As subtle and innocent as it was, I felt my heart pound in my chest.

I never knew he felt this way about me, but I was always too afraid to tell him I felt the same. I slid my hand between his fingers and looked over at him. I could only stare at him as he admired the clouds and leaves. I could see the reflection of the sky in his ice-blue eyes. As we lay on the ground watching the leaves and clouds, Artheus turned toward me.

"I really like you," he said.

"I think I really like you too," I replied.

"I wish we could be like this forever and ever," stated Artheus.

"Me too," I agreed.

Storm clouds had started to roll in, and rain began to fall. Artheus and I scrambled to the horses and raced back to the stables, laughing at one another for looking like soggy bread. Upon reaching the stables and dismounting from Dreamer and Despair, we both fell backward into the hay, continuing to laugh as rain dripped from our hair and clothes. A cool breeze drifted into the stables, but the chill was no match for our laughter.

Artheus stopped laughing when he noticed Aedon standing at the entrance of the stables. Artheus and I rushed to our feet and began removing the tack from both Dreamer and Despair. Without a word, Aedon just stood there with a stern look on his face. After Artheus removed all of the tacks from Dreamer, he took off into the rain without so much as a goodbye.

"Thanks a lot for ruining my fun," I said sarcastically.

"I was worried about you getting caught in the rain," Aedon replied.

"I can handle myself," I snapped back.

"Nathelia-" started Aedon.

"It's Your Royal Highness," I corrected to assert my authority. Aedon approached me with an even deeper scowl on his face.

"You may have been given that title as a birthright, but you have yet to earn the respect of addressing yourself as such," interjected Aedon.

"We will see what my father, THE KING, says about it," I threatened.

"He made you my ward because I am the only person he trusts with your life," said Aedon.

"YOU ARE NOTHING MORE THAN A LOYAL SUBJECT IN MY FATHER'S COURT!" I screamed.

"I HELPED SHAPE YOUR FATHER INTO THE MAN HE IS TODAY!" Aedon yelled back.

"You are nothing more than a washed-up old man who is hiding because you can't handle the heat of battle," I said, picking up a rake and pointing it toward him, but little did I know it would be a mistake.

"Try me," said Aedon, waving his hand at me.

I charged at Aedon with the rake raised high, but suddenly found myself on my back in the hay, with Aedon now holding the rake.

"How?" I wondered to myself. *"I didn't even see him move. But I know I can do this. I can beat him."*

I leaped to my feet and charged at him with all my force, only to feel the rake slip beneath me, causing me to trip. I shut my eyes and, to my surprise, I didn't hit the ground. When I opened my eyes, I was confronted by a towering pile of manure. The only thing standing between me and a foul-smelling disaster was the rake that

Aedon was holding. He had used it to keep me from falling face-first into the dung.

"Do you surrender?" Aedon asked.

"Never!" I declared.

Wrong answer. With a quick turn of the rake, I fell face-first into the steaming warm pile. Getting up to my feet, I was disgusted and humiliated. Aedon began laughing at my appearance. I was so furious as I stomped past Aedon back to the cottage. Aedon was nice enough to run a bath for me and took my clothes outside to wash. After I was dressed, Aedon began to cook a stew. He could see on my face that I wasn't amused and still mad at him. All he could do was grin in amusement.

"Come here. I want to talk to you," Aedon poke. said.

I stomped loudly across the cottage and sat down hard in a chair next to Aedon.

"I've watched you for five seasons and noticed how you have been with Despair," he said.

"And..." I said with a snarky tone.

"Despair works well with you, and I can see that you care for him, so I want you to have him," he continued. I was completely shocked by his words.

"REALLY?!" I exclaimed joyfully.

"Yes, he is yours if you want him," Aedon answered.

All the resentment that I had towards Aedon melted away instantly. I ran to Aedon and threw my arms around him, hugging him tightly. I'd always wanted a horse like Despair for my own. Having Despair was like a dream come true.

"What horse will you ride?" I asked.

"I was given another horse by your father," answered Aedon.

As the sun dipped below the horizon, I waited for my father's knock at the door. When darkness enveloped the sky outside, my father knocked urgently on the door, appearing rushed. I could tell immediately that something was wrong.

"Sweetheart, I don't have much time," said my father frantically.

"Father! Father! Aedon gave me Despair! Can you believe it?" I began with excitement.

"Yes, yes, Aedon told me he was going to do that," said my father. "I don't have much time. I need to tell you that I am going on a hunt tonight."

"But you will be back tomorrow?" I asked.

"Of course, my dear," my father answered.

Motioning toward Aedon, my father stepped outside with him. After a brief exchange of words, my father left. Unbeknownst to me, this would be the last time I would ever see my father like this. When I went to bed, I couldn't sleep due to all the thoughts racing through my mind. I kept thinking about how exciting it was to have Despair and how concerned I felt about my father's anxious behavior.

I watched as the sunshine rose through the window. Aedon awoke as if he hadn't slept at all, with no sign of fatigue or exhaustion. With Aedon awake, I got dressed and raced out to meet Artheus to tell him the news about despair.

"Artheus, you won't believe the amazing thing that ha-," I called out, but was cut short after noticing both Artheus and Dreamer were not at the stables. I did, however, notice Aedon's new mare standing beside Despair. After grooming both mine and Aedon's horse, I saddled Despair and raced to the tree where Artheus and I would usually meet. To my dismay, I realized that Artheus was nowhere to be seen.

I fled back to town as fast as Despair would carry me. In the crowded streets, I spotted Lady Agnes picking flowers from a local vendor. I stopped to ask if she had seen Artheus anywhere.

"His family packed up and left late last night," said Lady Agnes.

My eyes began to well up with tears. I couldn't believe he left without saying goodbye. I returned Despair to the stables and removed his saddle. Afterward, I began to walk slowly back toward the castle, but I stopped in my tracks after noticing two armored soldiers talking to Aedon outside the cottage.

My heart sank because the only person who could come to the cottage was my father. My stride turned into a sprint. As I approached, I noticed Aedon had his head hung low as he spoke to the soldiers. When I arrived, all three of them looked up at me with expressions of sadness on their faces.

"What's going on?" I asked with concern.

"I'm sorry, Your Royal Highness, but there was an accident when your father left for a hunt last night," one of the soldiers said.

"What accident?" I asked, worried.

"We aren't sure ourselves, but according to accounts from the soldiers that were with him, they had become unconscious, and when they came to, they noticed blood on the ground, and your father was not among them," said a soldier.

"Aedon, what are we supposed to do?" I cried as my heart was beginning to break.

First, Artheus leaves, and then I discover that the one person I cherished has gone missing. I felt a lump in my throat, and suddenly I was unable to breathe. I clutched at my throat, and my vision began to fade to black. I saw the soldiers scrambling around me while mouthing words that I couldn't hear, and then it all went dark.

When I finally came to, Aedon was sitting in a chair by my bedside. I sat up and asked if I had been dreaming, feeling a heartfelt remorse. He reassured me that I wasn't and that I had fainted. I buried my face into my hands and began to weep. I felt Aedon's warm touch on my shoulder, and it was comforting. It felt like I had lost everything that was true and dear to me.

"So what is it that we are supposed to do?" I asked with my speech garbled. "Should we return to the castle and await my father's return?"

"Not now. I was placed in charge of you during your father's absence," answered Aedon.

"But I am the princess," I declared.

"I am aware, but for now, I will attend to adult matters until either your father returns or you become of age to attend to them yourself," he stated.

"I am supposed to wait and see what is to come?" I inquired.

All I wanted at that moment was to hear my father's voice and see him walk through the door. I never realized how much I had taken having him for granted. I finally understood what I had because it was gone. Time seemed to stand. I didn't know if I would ever be able to escape this spiral.

Aedon did everything he could to ease my pain and alleviate my heartache. I started yearning for Artheus's return to escape the loneliness. Despite Aedon's efforts, I found it difficult to experience genuine emotional warmth from him. The sun had set and risen once more by the time I finally chose to go downstairs.

Aedon didn't pressure me to do my chores, but instead allowed me to sit in silence while I pondered the news I had just received the day before. Aedon prepared breakfast for me, which included beef, eggs, potatoes, and bread. I struggled to find the will to eat; my depression from the news had knotted my stomach to the point that I couldn't.

Aedon's face also bore an expression of sorrow, and I could tell that he was troubled by the news just as I was. As Aedon contemplated deeply with a cold stare into the blazing flames of the hearth, I could sense a rising tension of anger filling the room. Suddenly, Aedon stood and threw dishes into the raging fire. An expression of anger flickered across Aedon's face, which I found frightening.

I had never seen Aedon like this, and I had imagined him in this state during the battle. I pictured the fear of enemies as he struck them down. My heart pounded in fear, and my breathing raced. Aedon took notice of my fear as tears involuntarily streamed down my face. Aedon's expression changed, becoming more concerned and comforting.

"I'm so sorry, Your Royal Highness," said Aedon. "I didn't mean for things to overcome me like that, and for that, I extended my deepest apology."

"I forgive you. It was just so sudden…" I acknowledged.

"I should have convinced him to stay or return to the castle," Aedon said, blaming himself.

"There was nothing you could have said or done that would have changed his mind," I reassured.

"If I can't do so much as to protect the king, how am I to protect you?" Aedon stated with regret.

"You can scare the bejesus out of them just by being yourself," I said.

A smile began to creep across Aedon's face, and we found ourselves laughing hysterically. I needed this laughter at that moment. Instead of channeling our feelings through rage and anger, we found it more beneficial to transform them into laughter. For the time being, neither of us felt worried or depressed, and that alone was quite a relief given the circumstances.

"I think I needed that laugh," said Aedon.

"I agree," I said.

I discussed with Aedon the possibility of performing a search and rescue and how I felt lost without my father. Aedon had confided in me enough to share a story about how his father was killed by raiders and that he had learned his father was also an assassin. He informed me that he had single-handedly protected the king from a gang of raiders he encountered during one of his many travels to the castle, where he sold meat. Aedon also said that because of that moment, he was invited to the castle and became knighted. After being knighted, Aedon was offered an opportunity to train as an assassin for the king.

I asked him if he had any children or wives, and he told me he did not. However, he had loved once, and his late wife succumbed to a fever while pregnant with their soon-to-be daughter. Aedon had lost both his wife and unborn child to an unseen illness. I could see a tear beginning to form in his eyes as he spoke of them. My heart ached for him as he shared fantastic tales from his youth. I learned that he was a sheep farmer and that his father had been a butcher.

I was amazed at how a man who had experienced so much tragedy could remain so gentle. Perhaps I filled the void in his heart because he couldn't raise his own daughter. Perhaps I was his second chance. I wasn't sure, but I was incredibly grateful to have him with me.

Chapter 11:
Hell Hath No Fury

Five seasons had passed, and there was still no word on my father or Artheus. Aedon had become ill that winter and had become bedridden. I had turned fifteen when Aedon took a turn with his health. Soldiers would come and go to report that there still hadn't been any signs of my father.

The soldiers informed me that my father was presumed dead. It felt as if my whole world was collapsing. I had lost my mother, my father, and the first love of my life, who had also left. Three weeks later, Aedon was gone. A group of soldiers transported Aedon's body on a horse-drawn carriage through the snow, wrapped in the banner of my parents' castle. I rode alongside them on Despair.

The air carried a bitter chill that penetrated deep into my bones. My lips felt dry, and my hands had grown numb against the frigid winds. My eyes hurt as stinging tears started to freeze on my face. The pain I felt on the outside was nothing compared to the pain I felt in my heart.

I sensed my steed's uneasiness, as if Despair was aware of the circumstances. But of course, he could be, as he was bred for combat and death. Despair was both the most respected and feared horse among the soldiers, not just for carrying the most bloodthirsty soldier of the kingdom, but for his sheer fearlessness in the most heated battlefields.

Now, Despair was carrying me into a battlefield of my own. A battlefield of anguish and self-loathing.

With every step forward, my heart broke a little more. Despair carried me with unwavering strength and courage. I noticed the soldiers heading to an open field with a large pyre at its center.

What seemed like hundreds of soldiers on horseback encircled the pyre to pay homage to their fellow fallen soldier. The circle of horses parted to allow the passage of Aedon's carriage. I fought back tears as I watched Aedon's shrouded body be carried and laid upon the summit of the pyre. Horns began to blow in unison, and every soldier raised their swords to the sky.

When a soldier carrying a torch approached to ignite the pyre and the flames began to rise, Despair's demeanor began to change. He began to paw and stomp the ground, triggering a chain reaction that caused the other horses to follow his behavior. In unison and without command, every horse reared on their back legs as if to salute in solidarity.

I could no longer hold back the tears after witnessing such unity from both humans and animals alike. *This is it. This is exactly what Aedon would have wanted.* I glanced down and saw both Bane and Tyranny trying to mimic the behavior of the horses while howling a sad song. This act of unity demonstrated that Aedon was loved and respected by all.

I watched as the flames reflected off the frozen ground like morning rays of sunlight. I found the entire scenery peaceful, as if I were awakening on an early winter morning. The flames began to die down into a crackling smolder of ash and embers. Even with the flames extinguished, I could still feel a massive heat that reminded me of a hug I had once received from Aedon. I found it comforting.

As we left, I was pulled aside by a soldier whom I had never seen before. He was quite handsome but not as fetching as Artheus was. The soldier carried himself with strength and fearlessness. His hair was black like the midnight sky, and his face was youthful, but that of a man. Along his cheeks was a faint trace of stubble.

"I am to take you back to the cottage to meet your new counselor," said the soldier.

"And who exactly are you?" I asked.

"My apologies to Your Royal Highness. I am Aedon's nephew Xandor," stated the soldier.

"Very well, Xandor, let's go meet my new counselor," I declared.

Despite the sound of crunching snow underfoot, my mind was clouded by recent experiences I had endured. Upon arriving at the stables with Zandor, I spotted a horse that bore a remarkable resemblance to Dreamer. It couldn't be true. It seemed impossible.

Two soldiers stood on either side of the entrance to the cottage as Xandor and I approached. In a single movement, one of the soldiers stepped aside and opened the door for me. As I entered the threshold, I noticed a soldier across the room staring out the window. He was tall with short blonde hair. He seemed to have a muscular build, but also didn't seem much older than I was.

"I've always been curious about what the inside of this place looked like," said the soldier.

"Are you the one entrusted to be my counselor?" I asked with a hint of arrogance to assert my authority.

"It was my brother Aedon's final request," said the soldier. "Oh god, how I have missed you," he continued.

The soldier turned to face me, and my heart instantly raced. I gazed into his eyes. I knew those eyes. The same eyes I had dreamt of for years now.

"Artheus, is that you?" I asked, my eyes filling with tears of joy.

"Yes, Nathelia, I have returned," answered Artheus.

I ran across the room to embrace the person I had missed dearly for so many years. I leaped onto him, wrapping my arms and legs around him. We shared a long-overdue kiss. I could feel the long-lost, passionate embers reigniting into a raging blaze. Artheus motioned for everyone to leave.

With my arms wrapped around his neck and his hands gripping firmly under my buttocks, Artheus carried me up the stairs. He lay me on the bed and pressed his body firmly against mine as he began to kiss my neck. I felt his lips tease out gentle tickling sensations across my collarbone. His lips were as soft as the feathers of a swan.

Tearing away Artheus' armor, I dug my nails deep into the densely muscled flesh beneath his shirt. Erotic moans of pleasure began to escape my lips. I felt dancing butterflies all over my body with every soft kiss upon my flesh. Artheus disappeared beneath my dress, and the most pulsating wave of ecstasy passed over me.

I was washed in the feeling of his warm tongue dancing between my legs, followed by the feathering caress of his lips. Artheus grasped my hips firmly as both his lips and tongue drifted into a warm waltz between my thighs. Wave after wave of erotic bliss passed over my entire body. Involuntarily, I clutched my breasts and ran my hands across my body, following the waves of pleasure rushing over me.

Artheus brandished a dagger and sliced through the lacing of my corset, exposing my breasts. Gripping my breasts firmly in each hand, I felt his tongue caper around my nipples, sending electrical signals to my feet. Artheus grabbed hold of my hips and turned me onto my stomach as though I were weightless. His hands slid gently down my spine, followed by his lips, passing gentle kisses.

I felt a teasing bite upon the small of my back before feeling stretching pressure against my groin. With the feeling of a sharp, elastic snap, I was once again filled with a sense of warmth and wetness. An electric jolt passed over my entire body. As Artheus pressed his body against mine over and over, I felt him gently bite my shoulder. I had the tingle of a free fall wash over me in waves. With each wave, I found myself unable to speak or breathe.

I found myself only able to release gasps of air between each crashing wave of pleasure. With every thrust of his hips, the waves intensified, causing screams to escape from deep inside me. I was dizzy with pleasure and prayed that this feeling would never end. I watched as our shadows danced upon the wall, illuminated by the flicker of candles on the nightstand.

Our bodies were in perfect harmony with each other. My body tensed with every wave of pleasure, and I felt Artheus' grip upon my waist tighten ever so slightly. His grip was firm but gentle. With a massive rush of heat that filled my body, Artheus released a labored scream. I felt his body convulse and shake from intense pleasure as I felt a pulsating throb swelling in my groin.

My legs began to quake subtly but involuntarily. Flutters of intense sensations spread across my body like ocean waves crashing against rocks. Artheus collapsed beside me on the bed. Both of our bodies quivered in the aftershock of divine pleasure. Droplets of sweat were scattered across our bodies, and our hair was matted and damp. Turning to look at Artheus, I could see the pleasure-fueled glow of pure love in his eyes as they shone like light blue gems.

The glow of candlelight delineated the contour of his physique. We found ourselves enchanted by the presence of one another. I found myself in a state of bliss. My chest was pounding a love melody in my ears. I placed my hand upon Artheus' chest just to see if his heart beat the same. The rhythmic unison was in perfect harmony. Was this true love's duet?

I felt as if I were lying on a cloud—weightless and free of thought. For me, I finally discovered the feeling of freedom and security that my heart had yearned for all my life. For the first time, I had left behind any sense of regret that I had harbored deep within my heart and mind. I wanted this moment to last forever and the sun to never rise so that this moment could be frozen in time. Artheus ran his fingers through my hair with a look of admiration.

"I love you now as I have always loved you," he said.

"I couldn't possibly dream of a more fantastic moment than this," I replied.

"My heart ached in hope of the day to see you again," I stated.

"Aedon sent me to the castle to train to be a knight like him," Artheus clarified.

"Not only had you left, but I also lost my father," I informed.

"It was upon the news of your father's disappearance that the order was given for me to be sent to the castle," he answered.

"I can't believe Aedon wouldn't tell me," I proclaimed, sitting up in the bed.

"He couldn't because he knew if he had, you would have tried to follow, and Aedon could not risk you being in danger. He was always a protective older brother," Artheus stated.

"I still haven't come to terms with that," I said.

"That I left?" he asked.

"No, that Aedon was your brother," I answered.

"Oh," said Artheus. "Aedon told me that he needed me to learn to fight and to be able to protect you since his age was making it difficult for him to perform his duties," he continued.

"Aedon did his duties above and beyond expectations," I stated.

"Yes, he was a man of conviction and honor," said Artheus as a single tear ran down his cheek. Wiping the tear away with my hand, I leaned in and kissed him gently.

"I have a gift for you," Artheus announced.

After we redressed and descended the stairs, Artheus placed a sash over my eyes as a blindfold and led me outside. I felt the chill of the winter air sending shivers down my spine. After only a few paces, Artheus removed the sash, revealing the keep. Behind the picket gate, I noticed two wagging puppies. Both were Great Danes. Like Bane and Tyranny, one was female, and the other was male. The male was solid black with piercing blue eyes, while the female was gray with black spots and sharp hazel eyes.

"I heard the news that the dogs you had were great Danes, but their names escape me," stated Artheus.

"Their names are Bane and Tyranny, and they are wonderful protectors, but they are showing age," I informed.

"I hope this gift doesn't upset you, my love," pleaded Artheus.

"Nonsense! One could never possess too many precious beings like these," I clarified.

"What will you be naming these two?" asked Artheus.

"I will name the gray and black one Sophie," I declared.

"And I will name the white one Cerberus," stated Artheus.

"Then it is settled. Cerberus and Sophie, it is," I said with a smile.

Bane and Tyranny came around the corner to greet the puppies. The puppies began exchanging kisses with Bane and Tyranny, and all four dogs started wagging their tails. My heart warmed at the sight of the affection shared between Bane, Tyranny, and the puppies. Artheus and I took Bane and Tyranny back to the keep while heading to the cottage ourselves.

The sun began to set, and a grand feast had been prepared in our absence. This was the most food I had seen in a long time, and I was amazed by the spread before me. The table was covered with an array of dishes. Pies, cakes, and various other foods were scattered around the table. A carved roast sat at the center alongside loaves of bread. Fresh fruits and vegetables were also arranged around the table. The aroma in the air was nearly intoxicating.

"Where did all of this food come from?" I asked in astonishment.

"Don't worry over petty things like that. Just enjoy," said Artheus.

"Why is there so much food?" I inquired.

"I thought we could celebrate our reconnection with a feast. Only the best for my love," he answered.

Artheus and I sat at the table and indulged in the feast set before us. After we were unable to consume anymore, Artheus and I retired to bed. I lay in bed with him as we clutched each other in a lover's embrace. We just lay there peering into each other's eyes. I realized he knew about my capabilities. I would have traversed oceans long ago for the chance to experience this same moment.

I drifted to sleep, and my dreams of a happy future began to transform into a long-forgotten nightmare. I could see the mysterious man entering my mother's room. What was new about the dream was seeing my father walking behind him. My father looked different to me than how I remembered him. His skin appeared cold, and his eyes were dark.

"FATHER," I screamed, but my voice sounded like a whisper.

My father glanced in my direction before diverting his gaze to the floor. I tried to run to him, but the harder I tried, the slower I became. I stretched out my arm to reach for him.

"Not yet," I heard my father whisper distantly. The hall then lengthened, and the distance between me and my father grew.

"Why, Father? Why did you leave me?" I screamed.

"Wake up," whispered a distant voice. I closed my eyes to scream, and when I opened them, my mother was standing before me.

"WAKE UP!" my mother screamed, but I heard Artheus's voice. I jolted awake in a pool of sweat with Artheus sitting beside me.

"Are you alright, my love?" he asked.

"Yes, I'm fine. It was only a night terror," I explained.

My body was trembling in fear, and Artheus noticed it. He wrapped his arms tightly around me and held me close to his chest. Looking out of the window, I could see the sun was on the verge of peeking over the horizon. After Artheus and I decided to get out of bed, we both walked down the stairs, and he sat me in a chair in front of the hearth.

Artheus began to stoke the fire until, once again, it was a raging blaze. I took comfort in the warmth of the flames. I couldn't shake the thoughts I was having about that dream. Why was that specific memory placed to be that specific dream? I was deeply perturbed by all the questions I had pertaining to it.

Artheus poured me a strong cup of coffee and handed it to me. He also wrapped a warm blanket around me as I sat in front of the fire. Artheus sat in a chair beside me and rubbed his hand across my back. I had become lost in thought as I watched the fire dance within the hearth. I was quickly brought back to the present when Artheus spoke.

"What seems to be troubling you, my love?" he asked with the most sincerity.

"The dream I had, I can't grasp its meaning," I replied.

"What was in your dream that has bothered you so much?" he inquired.

"It was both a dream and a memory," I answered.

"Oh, how so?" asked Artheus.

"It was definitely a memory, but not the same as I remember," I answered.

"So tell me about this memory. Then you can tell how different the dream was," he said. "When I was young, my mother became very ill. I was called into her room by my father and was escorted by Aedon," I began. "Upon seeing her, she began to cough blood, and my father called for everyone to leave," I continued.

"So your mother had consumption?" Artheus asked.

"Yes, and I didn't want to leave, so Aedon picked me up and carried me out of the room," I answered.

"I'm so sorry,' Artheus apologized.

"Upon leaving the room, I saw an unfamiliar man entering my mother's room," I continued.

"Did you ever learn who the man was?" asked Artheus.

"No. After I saw him entering my mother's room, she disappeared," I answered. "But the new part of the dream was the fact that I saw my father following behind the unfamiliar man," I continued.

"Did your father say anything to you in the dream?" inquired Artheus.

"Not exactly. But I did hear him say 'not yet,'" I replied.

"Not yet what?" asked Artheus.

"That's the part that I can't quite figure out," I answered.

"Was there anything else you remember as being odd in the dream?" Artheus asked.

"YES! I noticed that my father did not look himself," I stated.

"How exactly did he look in your dream?" questioned Artheus.

"His face looked lifeless, and his skin looked cold," I said.

"Maybe you were envisioning the sight of your father being dead," stated Artheus.

"I don't know, but I can't shake the feeling that somehow I'm in danger," I proclaimed.

"Hush now, my love. You are in no danger as long as you have me by your side," he reassured.

A year had gone by, and life with Artheus was nothing short of a fairytale. We were married in the town church and rode out on our honeymoon on Dreamer and Despair. We were both set to be crowned as king and queen within the next fortnight. I imagined how proud my parents would have been if they could see me now. I had dreamed of becoming a queen like my mother every day since childhood. The dreams of days to come felt almost surreal. Every day, we would take the horses and ride to our favorite tree. On every journey, we would have Bane, Tyranny, Cerberus, and Sophie in tow. It was almost like being in a private parade.

Upon returning, Artheus would insist on ous going into the market so he could buy me a bouquet of flowers or a new dress made from the finest silks. He made sure that I never wanted for anything and that I was always safe. One evening, upon returning from our tree, my fairy tale life fell asunder.

We heard the chime of the emergency bells from the cathedral ring out in the air with haste. Artheus and I charged into town with the dogs in close pursuit. Upon entering the town, we could hear the screams of the townspeople as they flocked in a massive group near the center of the village. Artheus and I dismounted our horses and hitched them to a nearby post before pushing our way through the crowd.

As I pushed my way through the crowd behind Artheus, I started to discern the shape of a woman lying in the street. When I reached the center of the crowd, both Artheus's and my blood ran cold. Before us lay a woman dead in the road, bearing a striking resemblance to me.

A large portion of her neck had been torn away as if by some sort of animal, but one thing was missing. Blood. Where was all the blood? For a person to sustain such a fatal wound, she would have bled profusely. Her eyes were frozen wide in terror.

"We must go now! Quickly," yelled Artheus.

Before I could speak, he grasped my hand tightly and pulled me along to the horses with such speed and strength that I could have drifted like a kite behind him. Leaping upon Dreamer and Despair, we fled towards the stables. We quickly dismounted from the horses, and before unsaddling them, I found myself once again pulled behind Artheus.

"Lock this door! Nobody is to come in," Artheus barked loudly at the soldiers standing outside the door.

"Yes, sir," said both soldiers in unison.

When we entered the cottage, Artheus slammed the door with a look of panic on his face.

"Did you notice that-" I began to speak.

"Notice what? That the woman in the street had an uncanny likeness to you?" stated Artheus in panic.

"Yes," I replied. "What does this mean?"

"I don't know, but I take it as a message that someone wants to do you harm or worse…kill you," he said.

Artheus paced back and forth across the room in front of the hearth while lost in thought. I could see the worry and fear on his face.

"What are we supposed to do?" I began.

"Shh- I'm thinking," declared Artheus, holding his head up.

As the seconds passed, I grew increasingly worried about the situation. Artheus stopped pacing, put his hands on the mantle, and hung his head. I began to notice a sense of anxiousness coming from the dogs.

"We could increase the number of guards outside until this instance is resolved," I suggested.

"A handful of guards can only do so much. We need more than just a couple of soldiers," stated Artheus. "I need to be out there figuring out what did this and how to stop it."

"Bring the guards inside while you look for answers," I requested.

"Very well. I shall order more guards while I am away," Artheus began.

Two loud bangs came from the front door, and the dogs leaped to their feet, growling. Artheus withdrew his sword and proceeded to the door with caution. Gripping the door tightly, his sword at the ready, Artheus pulled the door slowly, but it flew open as the lifeless bodies of the guards fell inside.

Both guards had identical wounds to the woman in the street, with no traces of blood anywhere.

"You need to leave to go to the castle immediately," yelled Artheus.

"Come with me," I pleaded.

"Take the dogs with you. They will keep you safe," demanded Artheus.

Without a word, I rushed across the room and kissed Artheus before calling for the dogs to follow me to the stables. As I ran out the door, I witnessed chaos erupting in the streets. Men, women, and children ran frantically through the village seeking shelter. In a blur, a figure dashed across my line of sight, grabbed a woman who was running, and ascended into the air where she fell onto the cobblestone street with a thud. More and more villagers' bodies began to rain down, littering the streets with the droning thuds of fatal impacts.

Some were dropped onto the streets, and some fell upon the roofs of nearby cottages. Frantically, I ran to the stables to retrieve the horses for Artheus and me when a sudden urge to glance over at Artheus overwhelmed me. I stopped mid-stride to glance at him briefly and witness him being tackled in an instant by a blurred figure.

"NO!" I screamed as I tried to run to him for rescue.

"Help me!" cried Artheus as he was lifted into the air.

As I rushed to Artheus' aid, I was struck by a shingle from a cottage that had become dislodged by a falling body. With the sound of a muffled thud, my vision began to blur and fade to darkness. In that moment, I was unafraid of anything around me and completely unaware of my surroundings.

A crescendo of murmurs gave way to deafening screams as my vision began to return. Through blurred vision, I could see the silhouette of Artheus lying on the ground beside me. As the clarity of my view faded in and out, I was able to see Artheus lying on the ground with his arm outstretched and reaching for me. As I tried to reach for him, a dark figure appeared and ripped him away into the darkness. As much as I tried to resist, my vision faded into darkness once again.

Chapter 12:
As Blood Falls, Darkness Rises

I was once again brought back to the reality of my surroundings. I could smell the scent of smoke from burning cottages and feel its heat against the frigid chill of the winter air. When clarity once again returned to me, I remembered the fear I felt before I lost consciousness.

"ARTHEUS!" I screamed.

Sitting up, I could feel my head begin to throb. I felt weak and dizzy, but one thing was clear. I had to help Artheus. Forcing myself to my feet, I fought to regain my bearing. The town was in absolute chaos, with villagers running to and fro, screaming with wails of tear-filled cries. I had to know if Artheus was alive.

I began trying to walk, but stumbled with every step. The snow seemed heavier than usual, and my clothes were damp from the melted snow. I felt like I was walking on the deck of a storm-raged ship. My head was spinning, but I fought to remain focused. I couldn't think of anything other than Artheus. I needed to find him alive.

I made my way to the stables to check on the puppies and discovered a horrific sight. Dreamer lay slain in the hay of the stables. Her fur was matted in dark burgundy stains. Her eyes held a blank, lifeless stare. Despair had already been horribly traumatized by the events that had previously unfolded. Now, she was worse. She stomped the ground and reared in the stables. Her frantic neighing sounded more like screams than the sounds of a horse. Dark tear stains traced the curvature of her muzzle.

I wanted to comfort her so badly, but my head was spinning, and all I could think about was Artheus. My heart ached for Despair, but there was little I could do. I had a pitting feeling in my stomach that the outcome of the discovery would not be in my favor. I fought hard to remain focused on finding Artheus, but I was unprepared for the horrors that would await me.

Coming around the corner to peer into the keep, another horror awaited. A gruesome sight lay before me. Both Bane and Tyranny lay dead, mangled, and horribly disfigured, with their throats ripped from them.

Both Sophie and Cerberus were huddled in a corner, soaked in the blood of their brother and sister. Witnessing these beings mutilated and slaughtered without mercy left me mortified. The last thing I had from my father had been torn from me like a child from an unfit mother. I called for Sophie and Cerberus, who came reluctantly, still in shock. I embraced them both and tried to comfort each of them as best as I could.

They had their tails tucked behind them, and their ears were laid back in fear. Things were not looking good for me, and definitely not for them. I had never witnessed such a massive amount of tragedy and absolute horror. I began to find it hard to breathe as I took in the scene around me. What monster could have harmed something so innocent, so pure? I never thought of myself as perfect or saintly, but this was extreme.

My heart sank as I realized what I had lost. I became even more determined to find Artheus. I asked around the village if anyone had seen him, and I received headshakes and no's. I wasn't going to give up hope. We were destined to be together after everything I had lost. I was determined to find him. He had to be alive.

I saw Lady Agnes standing upon the steps of the church, tending to the wounded or dead as they were being carried inside. Pushing through the crowd, I made my way to the church. It seemed like everyone had wounds of one type or another. Seeing the mass amount of casualties, I feared for the worst and attempted to brace myself for it.

"Lady Agnes," I began to call aloud.

"Oh no, my dear child," she said.

"Have you seen Artheus? He's badly hurt, and I need to find him," I pleaded.

"I am so sorry, dear," answered Lady Agnes, trying to divert her gaze.

"Wha-...NO!...GOD NO!" I screamed in anguish.

My chest began to feel tight, and I found it hard to breathe. Once again, I felt the world around me spinning and racing out of control. My eyes welled up with tears, and my vision became blurry. I collapsed to my knees on the steps of the church.

"Where is he? I need to see him," I cried.

"You don't need to see him like this, dear," stated Lady Agnes.

I tried to run into the church, but I was stopped by Lady Agnes's arms. Fighting against the resistance that was keeping me from entering the church, I managed to break free from the hold that was preventing my passage. As I entered the church, my eyes adjusted to the dim light inside. I could see makeshift beds formed from pews being used to triage the injured.

The room was filled with the sounds of moans from the injured and cries from the families of the deceased. The outer walls were lined with bodies that were being covered in either cloth or painter's canvas. Blood had wept through the coverings.

Hysteria filled my mind. I tried to find comfort or answers among the religious paintings that covered the ceiling.

Lady Agnes had to be mistaken. I had just gotten Artheus back just over a year ago. I couldn't accept the thought of him being lost to me forever. But if it was true, then I needed closure. I knew what I needed, but I was unsure if my heart would allow it. Lady Agnes stepped beside me and placed a caring hand on my shoulder.

"Where is he? I need to know. Please," I said as I choked back tears.

"Are you sure this is what you want, my child?" Lady Agnes inquired.

"Yes. I have to see for myself," I reassured.

"This way," said Lady Agnes.

I followed Lady Agnes across the main cathedral to a side door that opened to a set of stairs. The staircase spiraled into a dark abyss. The stone lining the steps and walls carried the echoes of our footsteps as we made our descent. Wooden torches burned inside iron holdings along the wall. I could hear the sound of whispers passing through the air as we neared a long corridor at the bottom.

I began to make out the silhouettes of people gathered at the end of the hall. As I got closer to the end of the corridor, I could see clearly that the crowd of individuals standing there was, in fact, soldiers. Every head was hung low and resistant to meet my gaze. Reality began to set in as I stepped closer to the end of the hall.

Behind the soldiers lay a wooden door with iron plates and studs holding it together. Silence filled the air as I neared the door. The soldiers parted themselves to either side of the door as I reached for the latch. I felt a hand placed on my shoulder, and I turned to look at Lady Agnes, staring at me with a look of sorrowful pity.

"It's not too late to turn around, my dear," said Lady Agnes.

"I have to see this through, for me and for him," I replied, choking back tears.

With a nod, a soldier opened the door, and at first glance, it was just a dark room. I took my first step inside, and my heart started pounding as it continued to break, and my throat began to ache. I gained clarity as my eyes adjusted to the darkness, and I saw a room lined with shelves holding religious scrolls and manuscripts. In the center of the room, a single body was covered with a painting canvas, and faint traces of blood wept through it.

I was in both shock and disbelief as the rumors became true before me. I approached slowly, and my body began to shake with every step. With a quivering hand, I slowly reached for the edge of the canvas to reveal the horror underneath.

On the ground before me, Artheus indeed lay, cold and lifeless. His eyes were partially open, staring blankly. His pupils were dilated with no response to the flicker of the torch held by Lady Agnes. His lips were cracked and blood-stained, with faint bruising visible along his jaw.

By his positioning and the bruising on his neck, I could tell it had been broken. Most likely from a fall. A large portion of his neck was missing and appeared to have been ripped away from him before he died. The jagged flesh inside his wound had become a purplish burgundy color. His shirt was saturated in blood that had not fully dried. His fingernails were dirty and broken from dragging them on the ground while begging for his life.

I gazed upon him and watched the blood on his clothes glisten in the torchlight like rubies. I clutched his hand, hoping to feel any bit of remaining warmth, but all I felt was a numbing cold. I didn't want to let go and blamed myself for his tragic end. I begged to take his place instead. I would have given anything for the fleeting sound of his voice to enter my ears again.

I lay my head on his chest and prayed to hear a heartbeat, but no sound had made itself known. I couldn't believe the horror I was witnessing. After all this time, I was once again trapped in the feeling of loneliness. My body began to quake uncontrollably as my vision became a kaleidoscope of incoherent colors from the tears that formed.

"NO! You can't be gone," I pleaded.

"He was a wonderful man. I'm so sorry," Lady Agnes comforted.

My tears of sorrow began to grow into tears of rage and revenge. My emotions had become cold and vengeful. My jaw clenched tightly as I began to grow feelings of hatred towards whoever or whatever did this. Regardless, I would not let this go. I had decided that whatever was responsible must die.

"Whatever is responsible for this will die by my hand," I vowed.

"I understand you are having a hard time processing-," Lady Agnes began.

"No. I am accepting this my way, and I will right this wrong," I stated with gritted teeth.

"Let's not be rash and think clearly," advised Lady Agnes.

"I'M DONE THINKING! THIS WILL NOT GO UNPUNISHED!" I screamed.

My words reflected off the stone like shattering glass and reverberated into the outer corridor. I saw fear form on Lady Agnes's face. My voice carried like a haunting of ghosts without mistaking my words. I vowed that I would avenge Artheus, and any soldier who wished to stand at my side may join me on my quest.

"Lady Agnes, I need you to protect my secret," I instructed.

"Of course. Anything you need," she answered.

Lady Agnes followed me up the stairs back into the cathedral. As I made my way to the stables, Lady Agnes continued to the cottage. The sun had reached its peak as I readied myself for the journey that lay ahead. I saddled Despair and began to head towards the cottage. I made sure to be accompanied by Cerberus and Sophie. Before departing, I wanted to bid a final farewell to Lady Agnes.

"I am headed to the castle to round up the army to hunt down and kill whatever it was that took Artheus' life," I declared to Lady Agnes as I strapped Artheus' sword to my waist.

"I pray you learned all you could from Aedon and Artheus. And may your journey be brief and your revenge swift," she replied.

"I promise that it will be," I assured her.

"A being that is capable of this amount of atrocity is nothing less than pure evil," she said.

"That is why I intend to end its life because anything willing to inflict this massacre should be forced to atone," I stated.

With an affectionate but quick embrace, Lady Agnes and I parted ways. I mounted upon Despair and began my journey to the castle. I knew what I had to do, but a single question kept invading my mind. How? I had no idea how to deal with something of this magnitude and wished that my father were here to handle it instead. What would he have done? As my imagination wandered and I began contemplating ideas for how I was to seek my revenge, time passed relatively quickly.

With every victorious thought, my grip began to tighten on the reins. 'I'm doing this for you, my love. I'm going home, I thought to myself. Before long, the sun began to fade behind the horizon. I decided to take a brief break to give Despair a chance to rest as she was older now but still reliable.

As Despair began to drink from a stream and graze on nearby grass, I stayed watch and listened to the sound of nature. Cerberus and Sophie had stopped behind Dreamer, and both of them were panting heavily. The sound of trickling water, accented by the sound of birds and insects, was so melodic that if the circumstances were different, this would be absolutely blissful. But I couldn't allow things to be blissful for the sole purpose of my being here in the first place.

I began to swim through memories of Artheus, Bane, and Tyranny. I began to think about all of the innocent villagers and everyone slain viciously or wounded. I had a mission. An obligation as a princess to right these wrongs. How else are my subjects to trust me wholeheartedly? My plan was to find whoever or whatever was responsible and kill it. Simple right?

Cerberus and Sophie had accompanied me on my journey. Both of them chased insects and ran through the stream until suddenly, everything went quiet and still. An uneasiness filled the air. Despair and the dogs could sense it. Cerberus and Sophie slowly made their way back to me with their ears back, delivering low growls. I stood still as my breath cast a slight fog into the air. I tried to listen to the sounds around me, but I couldn't hear anything abnormal.

Despair had his ears thrown back and began stomping the ground. Quickly, I withdrew Artheus' sword from my waist and stood with my back to Despair as I peered into the darkness. That's when I first heard it.

"*Nathelia…,*" came a whisper in the air.

"*Natheliaaa,*" I heard once more.

"Who goes there?" I announced loudly. "Are you the one responsible for the attacks?" I demanded.

"*We shall soon be together,*" the voice hissed through the air.

Cereberus and Sophie's growls grew louder as they gazed into the night, scanning their surroundings. My heart began to pound in adrenalized fear. Both Cerberus and Sophie began to gnash their teeth at the sound of the voice. I was beginning to feel tantalized by the voice I was hearing.

"Face me, coward," I demanded. "Unless you are actually the one who fears me."

"*I fear you not,*" said the voice.

It sounded like it was coming from everywhere, and I began looking to the dogs to locate its source, but they seemed just as confused. The sound of my heartbeat began to pound in my ears like a thunderous drum. My hands gripped the sword even tighter. I could feel my knuckles whiten.

"If you aren't afraid as you so claim, then come out and face me," I called out into the darkness.

"But my dear, I am not hiding," said the voice.

"If you're not hiding, then where are you?" I asked aloud.

"HERE," said the voice, but it came from beside me.

I spun around to find myself face-to-face with the voice I had been hearing. A man. But not any man. This was the man I had seen years ago. The man I saw entering my mother's room when I was merely a child.

Those eyes that held a chilling, captivating stare pierced through the veil of my soul. I was paralyzed and unable to move. With a quick memory of Artheus, I regained control of my body and instinctively swung my sword for a killing blow. But to my surprise, by the time my sword was about to connect, I was only cutting air. It was as if the man had vanished before my very eyes.

In the blink of an eye, the man reappeared, grabbing Cerberus and Sophie by the throats, one in each hand. I watched as their eyes rolled back, and they struggled to kick free. He was killing them. I wasn't going to let that happen.

The man glared at me with a cold smile and carelessly dropped both dogs onto the ground. They started to gasp for air as life returned to their lungs. I stood there, horrified, watching them struggle to regain consciousness. As I watched, my rage, which had once been a dazzling fire, grew into a roaring blaze.

"You call these beast protectors?" the man taunted.

"Leave them alone. This fight is between you and me," I said through gritted teeth.

My body began to tremble with rage, and the grip I held on the sword tightened so much that my knuckles began to become sore. But I didn't care about myself at that moment. For me, my life was expendable, but I never planned to go alone. I raised my sword high and pointed the tip of the blade at the man with hopes of delivering a final blow, as I had learned from Aedon.

"Who are you?" I demanded.

"Excuse me for my lack of formality, but I am Corvainius," said the man.

"I'm here to tell you, Corvainius, that your reign of terror ends now," I announced with authority.

"Come and take your revenge," said Corvainius.

In a swift motion, Corvainius raised his foot and slammed it upon Cerberus' head, causing it to explode like a watermelon.

Horrified and sickened, I stood in disbelief at the events that had just occurred. Cerberus' body lay on the ground with a twitching jerk from his back legs, and a pool of blood encircled his body.

"THIS ENDS NOW!" I screamed.

Corvanius motioned with his hand for me to come forward, and I took it as an opportunity to carry out the strike I had planned. I rushed toward him as fast as I could. Before I could connect my sword to him, I saw, in what seemed like slow motion, Corvainius step aside. I could smell the scent of damp earth and decay from his clothes as he rushed past me and grabbed me tightly.

I was unable to move. He opened his mouth to display two razor-sharp fangs before I felt the searing pain of them being plunged into my neck, digging deeply into my flesh. I felt my life being drained from my body. I began to feel dizzy and weak as my blood was forced from my body, and a wave of cold enshrouded me.

What seemed like ages was only a few seconds as my body became drained. My hands grew numb, and I lost grip of my sword while being too weak to fight back. In an instant, I felt my body drop to the ground, and Corvainius disappeared from view. I remember hearing the sound of tearing flesh as Sophie drove her teeth deep into Corvainius' leg. With a thud and a whimper, I heard Sophie hit the ground.

My consciousness began to fade in and out as I lay on the ground, bleeding and fighting to live. I watched as the fog of my breath plumed from my body into the air. I found Sophie close by, lying on the ground, injured and exhausted. I crawled over to her and began to run my hand affectionately along her body.

"Thank you, Sophie. You did your best. Rest now, for I shall return, and we will finish this together," I promised.

Sophie whimpered in pain as she lay on the ground with no visible signs of injury. With every bit of strength I could muster, I crawled over to Despair and whistled with what little breath I had. After climbing onto Despair, I clicked my tongue, which left me in excruciating pain.

"T-Take ..me...to the c-castle," I panted.

With blinding speed, I found myself racing across the landscape in a desperate attempt to survive. I had to live for Artheus. For Bane and Tyranny. For Cerberus. And for Sophie. I had come this far and endured so much. I was not about to let it all be for nothing. They were counting on me, and I wasn't going to let them down.

The pain in my neck was unlike anything I had ever imagined. It felt as if molten steel was coursing through my veins. Not only was the pain burning, but the air also carried a chill that could freeze stone solid. Freezing rain started to fall as thunder and lightning rolled across the sky. The pressing force and chill of the wind made it hard to breathe or even stay atop Despair.

With unrelenting stamina, Despair continued to race against the storm to bring me to the safety of my castle. I could feel my life fading fast along with my consciousness, but I knew I had to hold on. The thundering pound of Despair's hooves began to lull me away from consciousness. My focus was regained with every blinding flash of lightning that crossed the sky like the reaching fingers of god.

I could see the castle in the distance, and it gave me hope. All I could think about was the horrific sight of Arhteus' body, cold and lifeless. I fought back tears that had begun to blend with the rain hitting my face. My heart was completely broken, but it became the motivation I needed to fight for my survival. The castle appeared larger than I remembered and seemed much more terrifying than I recalled.

Small flickers of light filled the windows like the eyes of a giant spider. There wasn't any reason to fear the castle, for I had been here before, but never had I seen it like this. The road leading to the castle's entrance lay littered with the remains of dead leaves. Even through my fear and pain, I knew I had finally done it. I finally made it home.

The lightning lit up what was only a silhouette, revealing the intricate details of each stone that had been laid to build such a magnificent structure. As I approached the castle's entrance, I saw the gate start to rise. Finally, I was safe, and I could close my eyes. As my eyes closed, I began to lose all sense of my feelings.

A wave of calm washed over me, and my pain faded into nonexistence. My fear of death disintegrated into nothingness. I didn't have a single feeling of worry or regret. I could no longer hear the sounds of anything around me, and at that moment, I didn't care. I was quickly greeted by the memories of all the deaths I had witnessed. I could hear their cries for help, and I felt an overwhelming sense of guilt, realizing it was too late to save them.

"Help us," they said.

Chapter 13:
Becoming the Devil's Own

I opened my eyes and found myself staring at the canopy of a four-poster bed. A large bureau sat in the corner of the room. I could feel the warmth of the hearth at the foot of the bed. A desk with a mirror sat next to the window beside me. Long satin curtains hung down from each side of the window.

A woven rug laced the floor in the center of the room. The bed I found myself lying in was draped in multiple fur blankets made from the pelts of various animals. A tapestry hung on the wall over the roaring hearth, containing my family's coat of arms. Taking in my surroundings, I recognized this as my room from when I lived here once as a child. The room seemed untouched by the cruelties of time.

I attempted to sit up, and I was quickly reminded of the traumas I had previously undergone. My neck was less painful, but hurt. The window had been opened to the storms, but I couldn't feel its chill. Turning my body to suspend my legs from the bed, I felt a throb growing in my stomach as though I were sick.

I was unsure whether I had been dreaming or if I had died, and I found myself in a false purgatory waiting for my judgment. I knew I had to survey my surroundings to better understand if I was in my castle or not. Once I confirmed it, I started searching for myself and discovered I still possessed Artheus' sword. As I tried to stand, the door slowly crept open, and I began to feel myself being carried across the room.

Feeling weightless and unsure of what caused it, I found myself in the hallway where pools of crimson and bodies covered the floor. I felt both horrified and calm at the same time. The idea of witnessing death seemed numb and distant to me. It was as if the trauma of seeing a corpse had faded, replaced by desensitization.

Unmistakably, I heard a voice calling out my name, and it sounded somehow familiar. "Nathelia." Over and over, I kept hearing my name being called, and I felt myself being pulled by an unseen force. "Nathelia." I wanted to call out to the voice I heard, but I was unable to speak.

Rounding the corner into the hallway, I saw a silhouette of a woman who looked strikingly familiar. "*Mom?*" I tried to speak, but I might as well have whispered. My voice sounded detached and distant, as if it were not my own. This had to be some form of a fever dream, or I was already dead, and I was being tormented in hell.

I knew my mind was probably playing tricks on me. My mother was dead. I saw her on her deathbed, and her weakness made it clear there was no chance of her survival. I wasn't aware of this as a child, but as I grew older, I learned to recognize the symptoms of consumption. I had learned that it was a terminal illness with no cure.

As I watched in shock and confusion, the woman appeared to levitate through the entrance of the grand hall. Just as I was about to call out, I heard my own voice in my mind speaking as clearly as if I had screamed. "MOM, COME BACK," I said silently.

"*Nathelia,*" I heard in my mind, but it wasn't my voice that I heard.

"*Why am I hearing voices? Am I going insane?*" I thought to myself.

"*We can hear you,*" I heard in reply.

"*Do I know you?*" I said in my mind.

"*Yes,*" said the voice.

I had to be losing my mind, or this was the most vivid fever dream known to man. It was official. I was talking to myself, and that is a sign of insanity. I wanted to wake up, so I pinched myself to see if any of this was real, and I felt pain in my arm where I twisted my flesh. I couldn't possibly be awake. This must have been a dream.

I once again felt my levitating body being carried down the hall. As I sensed myself being moved, I tried to find reason in the voices I was hearing in my mind. Parapsychology wasn't real; it was just a concept, wasn't it? My mind began to swim with inconclusive ideas.

I neared the entrance of the grand hall as I hovered over the countless bodies of lost souls filling the hallway. I began to feel afraid as I neared the entrance inch by inch. However, the fear I felt almost seemed welcoming in light of the events I had previously undergone.

"*Fear is a feeling, and if I can feel anything, then that means I'm not dreaming,*" I thought to reason with myself.

"*Correct, my dear, you are not dreaming,*" I heard the voice speak in my mind.

"*These voices aren't real. Nobody can hear my thoughts,*" I told myself.

"*We are able to hear your thoughts, and you can hear ours,*" I heard the voice answer in my mind.

"*Ours?*" I asked.

As I reached the entrance of the grand hall, I noticed how different it looked from my memory. The tapestries and banners were dull and torn. The stones on the walls and floor had lost their shine. The thrones that once seemed magnificent now appeared modest at best.

As my gaze swept across the room, I saw a woman standing in front of the window. She turned to face me, and I felt like I was about to collapse. I was speechless. It was her.

I hadn't seen her in so many years, but I remembered her so clearly that I couldn't have been mistaken. I kept telling myself I was either in heaven or hell, and that was the only way this could be happening. If I weren't dead, then I must be having a vivid hallucination caused by my wounds, or it was all just a fever dream. Either way, for the first time in many years, I was able to see my mother again in a nearly tangible form, rather than just in memories.

I lost all questions about why I was seeing her and was overwhelmed by the joy of being able to. I had so much to tell her, but I couldn't speak. I was confused about how she was here before me so vividly, as if she were really present.

"Mom?" I asked.

"Yes, my dearest Nathielia. I'm here," my mother said.

"Is this real, or am I dreaming?" I asked.

"This is as real as the cold of winter or the light from the moon at night," she answered.

"This has to be some form of hallucination, or I am dead," I stated.

"Not yet, dear," my mother responded.

"Wha-" I began.

"You will die eventually, yes, but not yet," My mother clarified.

"Then I am definitely hallucinating because twelve seasons ago I saw you...," I began to say.

"Die?" my mother interjected.

"Um…Yes, but," I said.

"Did you actually see me die?" asked my mother.

"Well, no, but you had disappeared, and we had known you were standing at death's door," I answered.

"Correct, my dear, my sickness was indeed terminal, but I was given a second chance," she stated.

"A second chance?" I inquired.

"Yes, my death was only the beginning of a life so extravagant that Bibles and holy men couldn't possibly fathom its splendor," my mother informed me.

"How were you given a second chance?" I asked, confused.

I felt betrayed. If this were truly real, then my mother had abandoned me and my father. For years, I had desperately wished for her to come back and would pray every night upon every star to send my mother home. I didn't understand then that her illness was fatal. All I knew was that she disappeared, leaving my father to place me in Aedon's care before he later had a hunting accident, which caused me to lose both of my parents. I thought it was selfish of her to leave us and never say a word all this time. I started feeling sick to my stomach, thinking it was because of the overwhelming stress from the recent news that my mother was alive.

"Before I died, I was approached by a man who offered me a second chance at life, but there was a catch," my mother said.

"A catch? A man?" I cried out in confusion.

"Yes, the man was a traveler by the name Corvainius. And the catch was that I had to leave behind the life I once knew for the safety of all I had loved," she explained.

"If you didn't die… Father had spent years searching for you… wasting time until he…," I said aggressively.

"He did what, dear?" asked my mother.

"Your husband, my father, died in a hunting accident," I finished.

"No, dear, he didn't die in a hunting accident," my mother declared.

The feeling of sickness grew stronger as my mother kept talking. Could my father have abandoned me too? I was overwhelmed with emotional pain. My heart had already been broken by the loss of Artheus and Aedon, but hearing my mother speak made it feel completely shattered. I didn't know how to accept what I was being told.

"What do you mean?" I demanded.

"I was there when your father died," my mother clarified.

"HOW? DID YOU KILL HIM? WHAT HAPPENED TO HIM? TELL ME!" I screamed.

"After I was given a second chance, I knew what I had to do, but it was so difficult to stay away, and once your father saw me in a crowd, I had to make a choice," she explained.

"What were your choices?" I inquired.

"Either kill him or make him like me," she answered.

Overwhelmed by nausea, I felt the room start to spin slightly around me. I had never been lied to before, and I wasn't sure if my mother was lying to me now. I wasn't sure about anything anymore. One thing I was certain of was that Corvainius had brutally killed Artheus. The monster had to die at my own hands.

"WHAT DID YOU DO? WHY DID YOU KILL HIM?" I screamed.

"She didn't kill me," said another familiar voice from behind me.

I spun around to see a man I once knew but had lost, and standing before me was my father.

"Hello, Nathelia," he said with a calming smile.

All I wanted to do was to collapse into his arms and weep like an infant, but I couldn't find the strength to move.

"What kind of dream is this? I need to wake up," I began demanding aloud.

"This isn't a dream, my dear," said both of my parents in unison.

"You're becoming like us," my mother stated.

"What is this? Some kind of sick dream?" I demanded.

"No, dear. You're dying," stated both of my parents.

"Becoming like you? If I'm dying, then that makes you ghosts," I said before I found it hard to breathe, and the room began to darken, causing me to collapse to the floor.

My body felt weak, and my consciousness was fading quickly. I was coming to terms with the fact that I was indeed dying. The room felt cold, and sweat was forming on my face. I watched as my parents stood over me without a hint of concern on their faces. I fought to stay awake with every last breath, and even though I kept my eyes open, the room grew dark and silent.

Silence and peace wrapped around me like a comforting blanket, and I surrendered to its sense of security. I felt a numbness wash over my body, as if I were nonexistent. I embraced the darkness and the quiet around me. I was calm and free from fear until I suddenly felt like I was drowning and needed to fight for air.

Chapter 14:
Battle Between Two Evils

Sitting up abruptly, I found myself gasping for air. It felt like it was the first breath I had ever taken. My vision began to return, and I saw my parents standing beside me with expectant smiles on their faces. My mother was holding a silver chalice in her hand, and my father reached down to help me get to my feet. Once I was able to stand, I noticed a pain in my stomach and my teeth. It was nearly crippling. My mother noticed my discomfort and offered me the silver chalice, reassuring me that its contents would ease my pain.

I took the chalice from her and looked at its contents. It held a red liquid with an exhilarating aroma. It was too tempting to resist, and I felt a strong urge to drink it. I started to sip from the chalice, and as soon as the liquid touched my tongue, a rush of unquenched thirst flooded my body. The flavor was sweeter than any nectar I had ever known. I was overwhelmed by its irresistible taste.

After I had consumed its contents, the pain I had felt before faded. All of my senses became heightened, and I felt more aware than I had ever been. The room, which had been dim before, now seemed bright and clear, with a bluish hue. I could see, hear, smell, and taste with a higher perception, and I wondered how this could be.

"What happened to me?" I asked as I looked around the room in amazement at my newly discovered senses.

"You are now a vampire like us," stated my father.

"A vampire?" I questioned.

"Yes, and you cannot die, but there is a cost to it," my mother answered.

"Cost?" I inquired.

"You must feed on the life sustenance of humans," my parents clarified.

"What life sustenance? What are you talking about?" I asked, intrigued but confused.

"Blood," said a voice from the entrance.

Standing at the entrance was Corvainius. His posture suggested he was unsurprised and lacked the concern to care. He seemed so nonchalant about being in the same room as me. I felt a surge of anger grow inside me as I stared at him. He was the one who attacked me, and he was the one who killed Artheus. He appeared bold, able to show his face after the horrendous atrocities he had committed, including turning me into a vampire. "Get behind me," I instructed my parents as I drew Artheus' sword.

"What do you think you are going to do?" asked Corvainius, smirking.

"You know what you did, and you must ATONE FOR YOUR CRIMES," I yelled.

"If you think you can take your revenge, go ahead, but you might want to ask your husband about that," stated Corvainius.

Corvainius levitated himself high above the room and crossed over me and my parents before lowering himself back down on the other side of the room. My vision began to turn red with rage before my focus was broken by a deep growl from behind me. I turned to see what had created the growl and noticed Sophie rounding the entrance to the room. Her eyes were as red as fire, and thick trails of saliva poured from her jowls. Her snarl was fierce as she snapped her jaws viciously. She walked slowly into the room and stopped by my side.

Somehow, after biting Corvainius, his blood caused a transformation in her. I believe she may have drunk the blood of those who had been slain in the hallway, completing her transformation. She wasn't a vampire, but she was immortal. Her loyalty to me knew no bounds, and for that, I was thankful. Corvainius began to show a slight twinge of fear upon seeing Sophie in her new state.

"This can't be; only humans can turn," said Corvainius, sounding confused and afraid.

"She hasn't forgotten what you did to her brother," I snapped back.

"She couldn't harm me then, and I highly doubt she can harm me now," mocked Corvainius.

I could feel the rage inside of me growing; I was consumed by an undefeatable urge to kill. My vision darkened to an ever deeper red, and my hands began to twitch. My body began to tremble from the feral madness I felt towards Corvainius. Before I took my revenge, I was going to allow Sophie to take her pound of flesh.

"Kill," I hissed to Sophie.

Her speed was completely unfathomable. In less than a second, Sophie had crossed the room, lunging at Corvainius. Corvainius was knocked back and threw his arm up to defend against Sophie's vicious attack. I could hear the crunch of bone as Sophie latched deeply into Corvainius' arm. He threw his arm back and Sophie was hurled across the room. With a hard thud, she slid back to my feet.

Sophie then gathered herself and got back to her feet. She rushed in for another attack. This time, she latched down on his hand, shaking her head viciously and tearing away a large chunk of flesh. Corvainius screamed in pain, and with blinding speed, he rushed across the room, slamming Sophie hard against the stone wall, leaving a broken dent in it. Sophie lay limp on the ground as her mouth dropped pools of Corvainius' blood.

My rage had reached its breaking point.

"That was a cute trick the dog did. Look at what she did to my hand. That actually hurt," said Corvainius with a sneering grin.

"You have yet begun to hurt," I said through gritted teeth.

I lunged my body toward him, and I saw the room blur past me. I was focused on him and him alone. I grabbed a hold of his shirt and, with one arm, threw him as hard as I could into the wall across the room. He collided with a deafening thud, sending pieces of broken stone careening across the room. Corvainius lunged back, projecting his body from the wall and grabbed me with a tight grip. I was slammed against the wall hard enough for both of us to be driven through it and fall to the floor in the hallway.

My body was racked with pain, and I found it difficult to even budge.

Corvainius was lying beside me, breathing heavily with almost the same amount of struggle.

Before I could bring myself to move, Coravinius sat up. He began to rise to his feet. Suddenly, a gray blur sped past me and smacked into Corvainius. I could hear growling and gnashing teeth as Sophie fought desperately to protect me. With a quick whimper and the sound of breaking stone, Sophie went silent.

Summoning all my strength, I rose to my feet and sensed my body healing. I felt more alive than ever, and the memory of the suffering caused by this monster fueled a fiery determination within me. I stood, staring into the shadows, ready for any movement. Corvainius emerged from the darkness with a limp, blood streaming from his arm and leg.

His clothes were tattered and ripped and covered in blood that I was sure was his own. He seemed exhausted and out of breath, but in a flash, he rushed at me. My enraged vision allowed me to see things in slow motion, including his supernatural speed.

I stepped aside and caught the back of his tunic before he reached me. I used his momentum to force his face into a stone pillar. A deafening crunch resonated through the room.

He lay on the floor motionless for a while, and I decided to approach him. I had a feeling deep inside telling me not to, but I was never one to argue with myself. When I got close, I realized the trap had been set, and I walked had right into it. I was too slow to avoid it, and in the blink of an eye, Corvainius grabbed my leg and sank his teeth deep into my flesh, nearly bringing me to my knees.

"AHHHH!" I screamed.

Before I could think of a counterattack, I was grabbed by the leg and hurled across the hallway. My body ricocheted from one wall to the other until I crossed the cold, hard stone floors. Struggling to hold onto my consciousness, I managed to bring myself to my feet.

Before I could move, Corvainius charged me again, but this time, he sank his teeth into my shoulder.

I fought to grab hold of him as I fell onto my back and kicked him away from me. I saw his body slam hard into the ceiling, causing debris to rain down on top of me. As his body fell rapidly towards me, I tucked and rolled out of the way, causing him to slam onto the floor. I caught myself and ponced to my feet.

Corvainius did not move.

I wasn't going to fall for the same trick again, so I decided to approach carefully. I could hear him gasping and wheezing on the floor. Then, I noticed the soft sound of pattering footsteps from down the hall. I looked up and saw Sophie approaching quickly. I reached down, rolled Corvainius onto his back, and saw a large piece of splintered timber sticking out of his chest.

I reached down and grabbed his tunic while drawing my hand back for a final blow. Sophie latched her teeth around his throat, and I could see bloody foam forming around her jowls. I knew that with a single motion, I could end this. I could finally have the revenge I sought after. I was doing this for Artheus, Bane, Bathory, Tyranny, and all the countless lives that were lost because of this monster.

"I beg you to allow me a chance to speak my final words," he said.

"Why should I?" I asked.

"There is something you should know," he declared.

"What should I know?" I demanded.

"Your…Your mother," said Corvainius, wheezing.

"WHAT ABOUT MY MOTHER?" I screamed.

"She did this. She made me turn you into a vampire," answered Corvainius.

"LIAR! SHE WOULD NEVER DO THIS TO ME," I screamed.

"She was the one that killed your love…Artheus," he informed.

"She wouldn't dare do that to me," I declared.

"She was threatened by you," he stated.

"Threatened? How could she have been threatened by her own daughter," I inquired.

"She never wished to give up her queenly crown to you and surrender her control of the kingdom. And since you are married, you would have taken the crown away from her," said Corvainius.

"She isn't like that, you don't know her," I stated.

"I have known her a lot longer than you have, believe me," Corvainius replied.

"You were the one who attacked me and made me into this, not her," I declared.

"She made you become sired to her," he said.

"Sired? What do you mean?" I asked.

Corvainius explained, "You drank her blood from the chalice she gave you, which transformed you into a vampire. Those sired by a vampire must answer to them."

"She only did that so I could have the chance to kill you," I replied.

"No, it was so she could be the one to control you. She demanded the attack on Blynehorn and said that Artheus had to die to keep you from getting crowned as queen and stripping her of her authority. She told me to turn you into a vampire because she didn't have the heart to kill her own daughter," he clarified.

"If it was she who wanted me to become a vampire, why would she have waited so many years?" I demanded.

"When you become a vampire, you never age, and she didn't want to steal the youth that you were destined to inherit," he answered.

"Why did you make my mother a vampire and take her from me?" I asked.

"I lost my sister many years ago, and your mother was the spitting image of her, and all I wanted was to have my sister back," he answered.

Even though I hated him and wanted to blame him, what he said was starting to make sense. I felt betrayed by my own mother, but I wasn't sure if what I was told was true. Could my mother really have been the one to kill Artheus? Or was this a trick by Corvainius to shift blame elsewhere? So many questions flooded my mind.

I ordered Sophie to release her grip on Corvainius and proceeded to drive my fingers into his shoulder. Even though he howled in pain, I dragged Corvainius back into the grand hall and slid him across the room to my parents' feet. He rolled on his back and began to cough up blood as he struggled to breathe.

"Say again what you told me about my parents," I ordered Corvainius.

"Your mother never intended for you to inherit the throne, which is why she killed Artheus," Corvainius said, struggling to find his words.

"LIAR!" screamed my mother.

"You had me turn your daughter into a vampire because you couldn't do it yourself," said Corvainius.

"Don't listen to him," my mother yelled.

"He said the blood you gave me was yours," I said.

"Yes, dear, that's true," she said.

"You sired her so she couldn't kill you to avenge her husband's death," muttered Corvainius.

"I'm done with you," my mother said.

My mother reached down, ripped the fragment of wood from Corvainius's chest, and drove it deep into his heart. With a single exhale and a solitary bloody tear streaming down his face, it was over. Corvainius was dead. He had said the same thing in front of my mother as he told me, which meant he had nothing to lose and knew he was going to die. The words I heard shook me to my core.

"It's true; what he said was true," I said, fighting back blood-filled tears.

"No, dear, it was all a lie. He was dying and had nothing left to lose by trying to fill your head with lies," replied my mother.

"Having nothing left to lose is why his final confession was true," I objected.

"So what if any of it had merit?" replied my mother with arrogance.

"I will kill you," I said through gritted teeth.

"Remember, if I die, then you die with me," said my mother.

Furious, I rushed across the room, grabbed my mother by the throat, and slammed her against her throne. I felt my grip tighten as I began to squeeze. I heard Sophie behind me growling and snapping, ready to attack. I didn't care anymore if it was my mother or not; I was determined to get the revenge I sought.

"Give me a reason not to do it. I don't care if we both die tonight," I snapped at my mother with my mouth wide open, ready to tear her throat out.

"ENOUGH!" yelled my father.

I felt his hands grab my arms and throw me across the room. I never would have thought my father would hurt me, but this was different. I never wanted to challenge my father, but he was the only obstacle in my way. Revenge and reunion with Artheus were all I cared about. I ended up on the floor next to Artheus' sword and grabbed it before pulling myself up. If necessary, I was ready to kill both my parents.

"Draw your sword, father, let's end this," I said, wiping blood from my arm where my sleeve had ripped on broken stones.

My father drew his sword and signaled for me to attack. I knew I had to stay clear-headed and remember everything Aedon had taught me. I couldn't let my anger cloud my judgment. As I watched, my father raised his sword to strike me by surprise, but I was ready. I brought down Artheus' sword to intercept his advance. Our swords collided with a bright spark, locking us in place as we struggled against each other's strength.

My father tried to use his leg to sweep my feet out from under me, just like Aedon had done many times before. I jumped into the air to avoid his move and then landed a solid right hook on his jaw. My father staggered backward, a look of surprise on his face.

"I see you studied the way of a sword under Aedon as well," he said.

"You have yet to see what I have learned, father," I informed.

For what felt like hours, our swords clashed as we matched each other blow for blow. My father was both impressed by my skills and determined to beat me. My persistence in keeping up with him gave me hope that I could win. We parted ways, both bloody and breathing heavily. Debris from all over the room was scattered on the floor after the relentless impacts of our bodies colliding. I thought my father had grown tired of the intense fight between father and daughter, but I was mistaken.

My father appeared to be lowering his sword in surrender, but instead grabbed a handful of debris and threw it at me. I turned my face to avoid any fragments hitting me, and before I could look again, my father took the sword from me and stabbed it into my stomach. With a strong push, I was forced back toward the entrance of the grand hall, where my father drove the sword through the wooden door, leaving me there suspended and bleeding.

"Now you will listen to me and listen carefully, Nathelia," barked my father.

"Spew your lies if you must. But end my life so I can be reunited with my love," I spat back.

"No, we are done with this blood feud. I am giving you a choice right now, and you need to think long and hard about it," said my father.

"Who are you to negotiate, especially when you are just as guilty of all of this?" I sneered.

My torso felt as though it was being cut in half, and all I could do was hold on to the blade to prevent it from slicing up my body any further. Blood poured from my hands as I held on and watched it pool under my feet. At this point, I was at my own mercy.

"Let me fill you in on how things have come to be," my father started.

My father told me how my mother and Corvainius met and why he took her. He explained how she had made a deal with him to become a vampire, in hopes of ruling the kingdom forever, and that she had convinced my father to join her. When they both became vampires, they took a blood oath promising that I would not be turned into a vampire until my eighteenth birthday, when I would no longer be a child. The plan to become vampires did not go as expected. They watched me from the shadows during all their years of absence.

They wanted me to become a vampire because of my mother's desire to continue being a mother. She wanted a daughter for eternity, not just a century. She did not want to watch me grow old and die without her. She felt that it was up to her and my father to always look out for me. She wanted us to be a family again.

I wasn't sure what to say about this, so I kept listening. My father told me how he and my mother planned to reemerge from the shadows and take back their thrones. They would tell a story of miracle healings and battles to explain their absence. I was to remain princess of the kingdom forever and marry after I became a vampire, not before. I listened to my father and started thinking about what my life would have been like if none of this had ever happened. I thought about how happy I was with Artheus and how unfair it was that his life was taken from me because of diplomatic jealousy.

I started to understand my father's perspective, but my heart remained broken. I was conflicted between the idea of reuniting with Artheus in death or being able to be a family again with my parents. I had to compare the truth with what I was told to determine if any of it really mattered. I looked into my father's eyes, and I could see sincerity in his gaze.

All they wanted was to be a family. Am I the monster for wishing to deny them what they had longed for over so many years? Am I merely a jealous creature who seeks selfish thoughts without considering others? Who is the real monster? Was it me, Corvainius, or my parents?

I had no time to reason through my internal conflicts; I had to make a decision. I was either going to remain a vampire and live forever with my parents as a family, finally achieving the dream I had pursued since childhood, or I was going to dismiss those notions as childhood fantasies and end it all for emotional greed. My body grew heavy, making it harder to hold my weight against the blade of the sword. My mind was made up, and the decision was final.

"I wish for us all to be a family," I gasped while fighting to hold onto the blade of the sword.

"You have always been loved by us, no matter how much you may feel as though you have to resent us," said my mother.

"From now on, instead of fighting amongst each other, let us fight alongside each other," my father suggested.

With a nod of agreement from me, my father approached and, with a single motion, broke the sword in half, causing me to fall to the floor. I lay in a pool of my own blood and watched as the wounds on my hands began to close. The bleeding stopped as my wounds healed, and I could feel the pain of my injuries lessen. Sophie walked over and sat beside me. She started to lick my wounds to reassure me that I would be okay. I rose to my feet, stood at the entrance to the grand hall, and looked around the room to admire the damage that had been done.

I felt ashamed of what had become of the grand hall. The thrones had been smashed and broken. Every tapestry that was hanging was in a tangled mess on the floor. The room suffered catastrophic damage, with windows shattered and stones completely broken, exposing the outer walls surrounding the hall. I decided to leave the remaining portion of the sword protruding from the door as a reminder of the night's events. Where Corvainius' body once lay, there was now only a scattered pile of ash and clothing.

The fire in the hearth had died down and started filling the air with thick smoke and soot. I checked myself, and my clothes were torn and ragged. Part of my dress had been ripped off, revealing dried blood on my leg. There was a large hole in the middle of my corset where Artheus' sword had driven through me and into the door.

My father's clothes were also badly ripped and tattered. His shirt had a long slashed hole that I caused. His sleeve had four long tears from my nails during the struggle. Both knees of his pants were ripped. Every tear on his clothes was packed with dried blood. He had dried blood on his face and along his ears. Smudges of dirt and soot streaked across his face and hands. Neither of us had words for wear.

After seeing the state of my father's face, I could only imagine my own. I knew he was impressed with how well I managed to fight back, and if I hadn't been fooled, the fight would have continued to a stalemate. Neither of us was left unscathed; instead, we were beaten, bloodied, cut, and stabbed. I was thankful that Aedon had trained me so effectively. I had hoped I would never need to use the training I received, but I was nonetheless grateful that I had it.

My mother stood with a slight look of shock and confusion. I could see on her face that she was impressed with my handling of a sword, but she was also disappointed that my father did not end my life in combat. I still held resentment towards her, but I knew it would only be futile if I pursued it. I decided to let bygones be bygones and learn to embrace this dark gift of vampirism. I had become the perfect weapon and killer among men. Perhaps my father would consider the idea of creating a vampire army to protect the castle against invasion. Or perhaps our people would accept the idea that we are superior beings.

Things were going to be very different from anything I had known before. The idea of possibly marrying someone and forcing them into becoming a vampire like me so I could spend eternity with them seemed farfetched and unlikely. I clearly did not understand if vampirism was a disease or a curse. I had a lot to learn from my parents about who I was and what I had become.

My parents and I spent hours discussing the lifestyle and capabilities of a vampire. I learned that, besides being pierced in the heart, sunlight was the only other thing that could be fatal for us. Since our bodies had died, fluids no longer circulated, so we had to consume blood to stay hydrated and prevent decay. Blood was less prone to evaporation than water, and its natural iron and carbon components protected our organs from rotting after death. That's why we specifically craved blood. We could also drink wine for its aged qualities.

I found myself unable to indulge in human blood when my parents and I would go out on hunts together. Instead, I would indulge myself in the blood of deer and cows in order to satisfy my thirst. Was it comparable to the taste of human blood? No, but I couldn't bring myself to take the life of a human. I remembered what I had seen the night of Artheus' death, and that would haunt me forever. Only once did I give in to the insatiable urge to drink human blood, and I nearly lost control. Had it not been for my father pulling me away, I would have caused a massacre. Upon that night, I had slaughtered fifteen people without any realization.

After my first taste of human blood, my mind shut off, and my body continued to feed from person to person without end or control. I felt terrible for the slaughter I had caused, seeing all of the remnants of twisted and contorted corpses scattered about due to my inability to control my hunger. It took weeks for me to finally gain control over my urges, and eventually, my parents assisted me by agreeing to only drink the blood of animals.

One night, I convinced my parents to accompany me on a hunt through the Blynhorn forests. I wanted to use it as an excuse to check on the well-being of those there who were hospitable and caring towards me. It also gave me a chance to glance at Artheus' grave beneath the tree where we would always meet. Even though he was dead and gone, I was going to make sure that his memory lived on.

One night, while hunting near Blynhorn, I took advantage of an opportunity that allowed me to approach the church. I made sure to hide my face under a cloak as I walked the streets at night so I wouldn't be recognized. When I arrived at the church, I placed my dagger, which was wrapped in silk, upon the steps. Attached to it was a note containing two words:

FOR THARIUS.

<u>*Coming soon*</u>

<u>*EIDOLON*</u>

<u>*SECRETS OF THE MONASTERY*</u>

<u>*CARDINAL SIN*</u>